JACK & JILL

KEALAN PATRICK BURKE

Jack & Jill Copyright © 2017 by Kealan Patrick Burke. All Rights Reserved.

All rights reserved. No part of this book may be reproduced in any form or by any electronic or mechanical means including information storage and retrieval systems, without permission in writing from the author. The only exception is by a reviewer, who may quote short excerpts in a review.

Cover designed by Elderlemon Design

This book is a work of fiction. Names, characters, places, and incidents either are products of the author's imagination or are used fictitiously. Any resemblance to actual persons, living or dead, events, or locales is entirely coincidental.

Kealan Patrick Burke
Visit my website at www.kealanpatrickburke.com

Printed in the United States of America

First Printing: December 2017
Elderlemon Press

ISBN-13: 978-1981371129
ISBN-10: 1981371125

For Adrienne
Who chased away the dark

"Won't you sit, in the light, where the sun makes jewels of your tears?
And listen for a spell as I pacify your fears
All you see is darkness, child; even as your shadow grows
And tries to stretch far away from you, to places you can't go.
And still you weep, still don't sleep, because of pain nobody knows.

Yes, there is darkness hiding in the wings
Yes, there are dangers that only night will bring
Yes, there are bad things that wish to quiet your heart
These are nothing new, my child
They've been with us since the start." - *Unknown*

"Jack and Jill went up the hill to fetch a pail of water
Jack fell down and broke his crown
And Jill came tumbling after"
– *Nursery Rhyme*

ONE

I DREAM.
My brother and I stand on the verge of one of two graveyards that swell up from hallowed ground to form lofty cross-studded hills overlooking the town in which we have spent most of our young lives. It has never been explained why the dead are buried at such a height, for surely it would make more sense to secret them away in some gated meadow in the valley rather than in plain view of the townsfolk, who could live quite happily without the reminder of what awaits them.

Mayberry has seen its fair share of tragedy. The people walk slightly stooped as if shouldering the weight of loss, their eyes cast downward to avoid registering the twin verdant rises that obscure the sun at dawn and dusk. There is a peculiar smell to this place, like a coat that has been hung up wet and discovered in a closet years later, a sense of age it is not old enough to have earned.

Gothic churches stand sentinel on street corners, facing taverns and pizza joints, and intimidating no one. The houses sag and creak in the shadow of gnarled branches that look like the arthritic hands of apathetic mothers. At the bandstand, stubbornly holding court between a Romanesque town hall and a bank, and looking out over a concrete lot long awaiting development by a planning committee who no longer cares, sits a violinist, who makes up songs as she goes. Her music fills the air, and she never repeats a tune.

This is our town.

I am twelve, John is nine, and we have not yet learned of death. Pain and horror, however, are kindred. They visit us nightly, and take away little pieces of our soul. We live in nightmare and escape during daylight. And we do it here, in a cemetery that reaches in supplication to the sky, its base ringed with dark mausoleums.

We stand atop the hill, looking down at the long steep slope devoid of graves which leads to the road, and beyond, to the low-slung form of a prison that awaits us in a scant few weeks—the elementary school. We come here every day, and we engage in a ritual so childish and uncomplicated, it allows us to remember who and what we are, or at least, what we're supposed to be. What we wish we were.

"Ready?" John asks, a wide smile on his pallid young face. The breeze makes his sandy hair dance. He is wearing his navy-colored dress pants and a light blue shirt rolled up at the sleeves. A navy tie hangs loosely from his neck. I am wearing a pretty white dress with red polka dots and my white Mary Janes. Mother calls these outfits our "Sunday Best" and she will not be happy when we ruin them, but neither of us care. Mother has been too selective in the things that concern her, and the guilt of that will lessen the severity of any reprimand.

"Ready," I reply, and in tandem, we take a few steps forward.

I am vaguely aware of a man, little more than a hunched shadow, sitting down there on the wall that separates the grass at the bottom of the hill from the road. His back is to us, his attention fixed on a newspaper, as unconcerned with us as we are with him.

We drop to the ground. The grass is still damp from the morning dew. As mother fretted after we exited the church earlier, our skin and clothes will be stained, but this is welcome, if only to obscure the invisible, more permanent stains of which we are always so intimately aware.

We lie on our backs, our feet almost but not quite touching, arms close to our sides.

"Go!" John yells, and we roll down the hill. Though my brother's name is John, and mine Gillian, between us we are Jack and Jill. It is a fantasy, an escape, a secret identity no one can touch, further strengthened by this weekly ritual.

I can never understand why, when we start out together from the same place, John somehow always manages to get ahead of me.

Today is no different.

Faster and faster we go, the world spinning crazily in my vision, which is little more than snatches of green and sky and flashes of light and dark blue as John shrieks with delight. Here and there the ground is unpleasantly stonier as I tumble over rocks half-buried in the earth, bruising my elbows and knees and scraping my skin. I don't care. I feel nothing but elation. My flesh tingles, the grass whispers against my face. Dew wets my lips. I close my eyes and it is as if the world is moving and I am lying still.

It goes on forever, dream-time stretching to delay the imminent horror.

And then it comes.

I reach the bottom and stop. Lie on my back, breathless. Moisture seeps through my dress as I look up at the whirling sky, which has grown darker since we began our descent. Ugly gray clouds seep over the hill, infecting the blue, and with it comes a chill.

An involuntary moan escapes me. It makes no sense in the dream, for I have not yet discovered the source of the latent dread. Perhaps it is my adult self protesting the direction in which my subconscious is bound.

My skin crawls, but for now I can do nothing but watch the darkening sky, which seesaws over and back as my vision tries to settle.

A sky-spittle speck of rain hits my cheek. My heartbeat thunders in my ears, competing with the hollow sound of my own breath bellowing in and out of my lungs.

I tell myself this is why I can't hear John.

Gradually, I roll over on my side. I look at the school. The windows are black, neither reflecting the world nor showing what might exist within. I feel a vague tightening in my gut at the thought that soon it will consume us. To the right, I note that the man is gone. Further right, John is sprawled on his back, arms splayed out as he too stares up at the sky.

Unsteadily, I get to my feet, black sparks pulsing in my vision. I fear I might be sick, but close my eyes and allow the last of the disorientation to pass.

"You win," I call to John, because even though I'm not sure which one of us reached the bottom first, it is safe to assume it wasn't me. Besides, there is no competition here. There never is. I love John more than anything else in the world. Alone, the events we've been forced to endure would have destroyed us. Together, we can find solace in a world that seems to shun it.

There is blood on the grass.

I stop walking as more rain pats my face, not yet able to fully register the long thin shadow that edges its way into my periphery as the man I thought was gone reappears.

The blood, an odd color, more like bad movie blood than anything I have seen in real life, forms a thick wide ragged carpet leading from halfway down the hill to where John lays unmoving three feet away.

The man waits, in no hurry for me to discover his handiwork, and I am in no hurry to look upon him. I know who he is.

"John?"

I step closer to my brother.

Ferocious agony locks my chest and I drop to my knees in grief. I've been here before, though the horror never gets old. I know all too well the pattern of this malignant dream and my throat closes, trapping a scream. My breath catches. I try to close my eyes, and find that I can't.

The stump of John's neck paints the grass crimson.

My heart crashes against my ribs. Bile fills my mouth.

Fear and terror turn to rage, as I finally look to my right, to the thing awaiting my attention. I do all of this because it has been rehearsed, practiced a thousand times over twenty-odd years of dreams.

The man is tall and thin, and though a clear plastic bag has been wrapped tightly around his badly decomposed head, I recognize his face.

It is my father, and his mouth is wide open, filled with maggots that tumble free only to be trapped again in the folds of the bag. They move languidly against the plastic.

He is wearing a funeral suit stained with dirt. His white shirt and bare feet are spotted with my brother's blood.

I weep and bring my hands up to cover my eyes, but they too are made of plastic and hide nothing. Certainly not the gruesome gleeful bobbing of my father's suffocated head, nor the senseless fact that he has rusted clothes hangers for hands. Like a fish, John's head has been hooked through the roof of the mouth on one of them. His handsome little face now looks like a poor imitation, absent in death of everything that made it beautiful in life.

Finally, the scream escapes, a train of utter anguish that plunges free into the cold air. It is mimicked by a peal of thunder as the sky splits and the rain falls in sheets that have more weight than is natural. I am soaked in an instant. Rising from my knees feels like I am struggling to stand underwater.

The plastic bag turns a foggy gray as hurried, excited breath obscures my father's face. Behind and above him, darkness rushes across the gravestones, creeping down the hill like spilled oil.

He raises the unburdened clothes hanger to show it to me and I hear his voice inside my head. Such a good girl. Do you remember how it felt to have it inside you? Twisting? Turning? It takes guts to know, and I know your guts. Such a good girl.

TWO

"YOU LOOK LIKE HELL," Chris said, shoving a cup of black coffee before me.

"Morning to you too," I replied. I hadn't had a drink in eight years, but I remembered the hangovers vividly, and this felt like one. The golden sunlight streaming through the picture window behind my husband illuminated every speck of dust in the room and seared my brain, making my temples throb with the beginning of what promised to be a skull-splitting headache by noon. "Can we draw the blinds?"

"Sure." Chris yanked the string, closing the Venetians midway. It narrowed the light into isotropic bars. Not nearly enough to force the pain into submission, but it would do for the time being. "Quite a song-and-dance routine you performed in bed last night." He settled down at the table close to me. There was an amused look on his face that belied the concern in his eyes. "The nightmare again, I'm guessing?"

I nodded, sipped at coffee that scalded my tongue. The pain was a welcome distraction and dissipated some of the fog.

"This can't keep going on, babe. How many nights this week has it been that you've ended up Riverdancing yourself out of sleep?"

I shrugged, even though I knew exactly how many.

"You may want to talk to someone."

Right now, I don't even want to talk to you, I thought, and gave him a withering look. "About a dream? Suddenly we have the money for an overpriced shrink to try to analyze subconscious brain-junk? When did that happen?"

"If it was just a dream, that would be something," he said, pausing to take a bite of his bagel. A dot of cream cheese clung to his lower lip. I remembered when I'd found that endearing, might even have kissed it away. Now I had to avert my gaze because I found it vaguely repulsive. "But it isn't. Nightmares aren't supposed to be persistent. And considering the content of yours, it's obvious you need to resolve something. Or have it resolved for you."

"You doing a correspondence course in psychotherapy now? There's nothing to resolve. It's a nightmare, that's all."

"One that's costing you your sleep."

"I'm sure it's natural for cases of my kind." Although I hadn't described in length what had happened to me as a child, Chris knew I'd been abused, and that associated nightmares had plagued me for most of my life. His reaction had been somewhat typical. He'd wanted to track my father down and beat him to death. As a result, I had kept from him the fact that my father still lived in Mayberry, which was less than an hour from our old farmhouse.

"Yeah, but that's just it. You're not a *case* anymore. Why not just go and get a prescription for sleeping pills or something?"

"I tried that, remember?"

"*Hardcore* pills. Something that'll induce a temporary coma if it means you'll get some rest."

"Sleeping's not the problem, Chris. Waking up is."

"Well, I'm worried about you. You haven't had a good night's sleep in months. You're losing weight, you look run down, your moods are all over the place, and if you call off work one more time, they're going to fire you."

I waved a hand at him in disgust. "All right, Jesus. It's too early for this." *And what the fuck*, I asked myself, *qualifies you—a goddamn bank teller—to analyze or dictate how I deal with my dreams anyway?* It was an uncharitable thought, and I realized this, but simply being aware of the venom did nothing to drain it so I focused on my coffee.

"Sorry." He sighed. "So, what was the dream about last night?"

"The usual. I really don't want to talk about it." Right at that moment, I was determined not to give the dream any more attention than it deserved. The light of morning should have been comforting, but it wasn't, no more than it would have changed the aesthetic appeal of roadkill.

Silence fell between us.

If I was honest with myself, I'd have admitted that he was right about the moods, of course, and the exhaustion. I was so tired I could hardly think straight anymore. Maybe therapy would have helped, but I doubt I'd have let it.

After what my father was doing to me and John came out, among the strangers who'd come to our house armed with notepads, coloring books and fake smiles, was a child psychologist named Doctor Raymond Scott. The irony was that nobody had ever thought of my father as monster, because he didn't look like one. On the surface he'd been a kind, jack-of-all-trades and glad to let you borrow whatever tools you need type, a salt of the earth good 'ol boy who would stop to pick up a hitchhiker no matter how inadvisable it was to do so simply because he remembered what it had been like having to ride his thumb to work when he couldn't afford a car. A staunch Republican who'd said "Hell yeah!" to our invasion of foreign territories and festooned the back of his truck with Pro-War bumper stickers. A man who'd been good to his kids, a man with a benevolent face. No, it was madness to think he could do such terrible things. But he had. Conversely, Doctor Scott, the state-appointed Good Guy, had looked like just the kind of sicko who would lock himself into a bathroom with a small child and whisper sweet, soothing things to them as he caressed their flesh in ways his unnatural hunger could not quite aid him in disguising as tender. But he wasn't. *He* was the Good Guy.

But then, to us, in those dark days, everyone was a monster, and everyone wore a mask to hide the fact. Adults could not be trusted.

"Look," Chris said, putting his hand on my arm. "You deal with it however you see fit. I'm just concerned, that's all. I don't want you getting sick over this."

"I know," I muttered. "I won't."

He rose and dumped his cup and plate into the sink. *For me to take care of*, I thought, irritably.

"Where are the kids?" I asked, if only to change the subject.

"Bus picked them up about fifteen minutes ago. You just missed them. They said to tell you good morning, Mommy." He smiled as he said that, but I imagined there was a hint of accusation there too, as if he believed I should have been there to see my children off. Ordinarily I was, but lately, since the frequency of the nightmares had increased, things had been different.

"Probably the bus that woke me," I said, by way of dismissal.

He watched me carefully for a moment. Then: "Tell me what I can do to make this better for you, honey."

Honey. A word that had never bothered me before, but was like cold water dumped on my neck now. I felt compelled to point this out, but the sincerity of the love in his face dissuaded me. Later, maybe, if the sleep didn't blunt the edge, I'd ask him nicely never to say it again. And to start washing his own fucking dishes.

"I just need to rest," I explained. "It comes in waves. Usually if I'm stressed."

"What's stressing you?"

"Nothing specific. Just a combination of little things. Work, mostly."

He approached me on a wave of Aqua Velva cologne that turned my stomach, and kissed me on the top of the head, the same way, I noted, that he kissed our children, as if we all required the same level of attentiveness to make our *owies* better.

"Well, if I can help relieve any of that stress, you let me know."

"Sure."

He squeezed my shoulder, then went to the counter and scooped up his keys. "Well...I'm off. Try to take it easy today, okay?"

"You know I will." I gave him a little finger-wave.

"See you at six?"

"You bet."

"Love you."

"You too."

Then he was gone and the house settled around me, quiet and still. Expectant.

I waited until I heard Chris's car pull out of the driveway, then went to the window and shut the blinds all the way.

Though it shouldn't have been, the gloom was comforting.

After washing down some Advil with orange juice, I retreated to the couch, grabbed the TV remote and killed the histrionic protestations of some bizarre-looking cartoon dinosaur as a caveman walloped him with a club.

I was glad to be alone.

In minutes, I was asleep.

THREE

I DREAM.

Downtown, and ragged shadows fly blackly across the facades of the buildings and the narrow potholed road that winds between them as if the street has become a screen for a monochromatic kaleidoscope. The cars parked on either side of me are empty and coated with a fine layer of dust or ash. I have fled the hill with no memory of my passage. There has been no discernible transition between locales. No memory of running. I am simply here, alone, and yet not.

For one, my father is following, though when I look back over my shoulder I see no sign of him on the hill. But I can feel him, can almost hear him talking to my brother, chiding the vociferousness of the severed head when it should know by now the importance of silence.

Hush now, someone will hear.

For another, in every building there are people in the windows. Men, women, children, but they have their backs turned away from the street, away from me and the nightmare that is mine alone. They stand frozen in place, staring forward. I know they are not looking at anything, and that is the point, because looking at nothing means they're not looking at me, not bearing witness to the atrocity. And if they can't see it, they can't be responsible for whatever comes of it. I open my mouth to scream for their help, and only the wind emerges — an autumn wind that sends rust-colored leaves scratching along the gutters to be swallowed by storm drains that have curved into hungry smiles.

One of John's Matchbox cars, a red Corvette, trundles its way along the gutter to my right and overturns, wheels spinning uselessly when it collides with the barrier of a discarded rain-sodden Bible.

God sees all. *My father's words, echoing in my head.* **And God approves.**

The clouds are filthy, carelessly painted on a sky pierced by the spires of twin churches.

It is to the nearest of these churches—my church—that I run. My body jolts as my feet pound the fissured asphalt, the low whine of fear from my throat sounding like a distant car alarm to my ears. In the corner of my eye, I see that some of the cars are not empty after all. Hunched shadows rock back and forth in the passenger seats, like children impatiently awaiting drivers. I turn my head away, afraid to look directly upon them, and see a woman in the window of a bookstore. She is wearing a stained apron over a floral-print dress and the skin on her forearms is blanched with flour. Her hands are by her sides. I can't see her face, because like the others, she has her back to me, but I know by her costume and the slope of her neck, exposed beneath the cruel knot of a bun of steely gray hair, that she is my mother.

The ache in my heart at the sight of her does nothing to slow my progress.

Like the others, she has no help to offer.

Unlike the others, she knows it is expected of her, that it is her duty.

And still she looks away.

In another window, a rotund black-haired woman in a hideous dress stands flanked by four children of various ages. They are turned away, but she is not. Instead, she stares sadly at me, and mouths words I can't understand. Mrs. Farris, I realize, and I am stricken with self-pity and terror that threatens to drain the urgency from me.

But then a sound from somewhere behind infuses my flight anew. I risk a look over my shoulder and see my father yanking open the door of one of the cars. He no longer holds John's head in his hooked hands. Now he holds only the car door as he bends down to peer in at the occupant.

The cold gray light makes the plastic bag over his face look like a swatch of dirty cloud.

In the passenger seat the hunkered shadow bobs excitedly and screams with the sound of discordant violins that never play the same tune twice.

I look away as that sound is rent into staccato rhythms by the monster's ministrations and focus on the church, which seems so tantalizingly close and yet impossibly far away.

The dream skips, mercifully, and I am standing before the church. It towers over me in judgment, its spire appearing gelid, like a black tentacle probing the bottomless depths of the sky. Over the massive doorway—surely big enough in the dream for God himself to enter—is a mosaic that in life depicts a haloed St. Peter looking appropriately mournful in his service to the Almighty, reading from a book with a cross emblazoned on the cover, as a tropical bird of some indeterminate breed looks impassively on. But, in adherence to the law of nightmare, the mosaic does not show anything so benign now. Instead it depicts a crimson sun in the background, the thick lines radiating from the blood-red orb better suited to a cereal box illustration. In the foreground are figures that must represent John and me. We are facing each other, our hands raised, palms pressed together as if frozen in the act of playing pattycake. We are wearing clothes that might have been in fashion a hundred years before I was born. Our faces are smooth, featureless orbs like the faces of art-class mannequins. No eyes, no nose, no mouth. And between us and the sun stands a figure on a hill, a man with hooks for hands and a plastic bag over his head that is filled with red light. The shadow he casts, however, is not that of a man, but a crude diagonal X-shape that stops just short of the children, of us.

With the sound of a tree falling, the church door opens and there is blackness inside.

Unable to take my eyes from the strange mosaic, despite the Stygian darkness before me and the prickling of the hairs on the back of my neck *that tells me my father has been standing behind me all along, perhaps looking with equal curiosity at the scene above the door, I hurry inside.*

In the womb of the church I am blind as the door slams shut.

FOUR

SAM, MY NINE-YEAR-OLD, WOKE ME.
"Mommy!"
Behind him stood my eldest child Jenny, looking sullen, her book bag like a sleeping dog at her feet.

"Hi," I murmured and sat up. My neck ached from sleeping without a pillow and I winced as I worked out the kinks. "Time's it?"

"Four-thirty," Jenny droned. "Why were you sleeping?"

"Why not?" I asked, unappreciative of her attitude before I'd had a chance to prepare for it.

"It's *day*time." She folded her arms, looking much like her father did when he disapproved of something I'd done. As he did often. Daddy's little girl.

"I haven't been sleeping well."

"That's because you stay up too late."

I rubbed a hand over my face and felt the slimy wetness of drool on my chin. *Beautiful.* Fragmented images and emotions from the nightmare clung like cobwebs to my brain. My head throbbed. "Jenny, don't you have homework?"

"*I* don't!" Sam enthused and gave me a delighted grin. "Teacher was out sick! We had a substitute."

I gave him as much of a smile as I could muster and tousled his light blond hair. "That's good. You want to watch some TV?"

"Uh-huh. S'why I woke you."

Amused, I nodded and handed him the remote. "Knock yourself out, kiddo. But keep it down, okay? Mommy's head hurts."

"Mommy's head *always* hurts," Jenny mumbled.

She hadn't moved from the door. I frowned at her. "What's with the attitude?"

She shrugged. "What's with *your* attitude?"

I closed my eyes briefly. Wished Chris was here to deal with this shit. "Are you going to tell me what's wrong or am I supposed to guess?"

"Why? It's not like you care."

"Why would you say that? Of course I do." Despite wanting nothing more than another lethally strong cup of coffee and maybe a long walk to clear my head, I patted the seat next to me. "Come here."

She shook her head, bit her lip. "I want Dad."

"He's not here. Won't be for a while yet."

"I don't care. I want him."

"I'm here. You can talk to me."

"No." The hurt in her eyes was astounding, and worrying.

"Jenny..." I started to say, but then Sam cut in, one small forefinger pointed in accusation at his sister.

"You're crying," he announced, beaming. "Big baby!"

"Shut *up*, you little retard," Jenny screamed and crossed the distance between her and her brother with blinding speed, her arm jerked back, palm raised in preparation to strike him. She was trembling, and I knew that if that blow met its target, it was going to hurt. As her hand came down in a vicious arc, I intercepted it, grabbing her wrist a little too hard. Sam scooted backward, no longer afraid of his sister's violence toward him, but of whatever dynamic my preventing it would cause.

Jenny glared at me, her fourteen-year-old face contorted with a mixture of agony and rage, the latter being the predominant emotion. "Let me *go!* I *hate* you. I want *Daddy!*" She jerked in my grip, struggling to pull away from me, her feet digging into the carpet.

"Jenny, stop," Sam said quietly, alarmed by her temper.

"I understand you're upset about something," I told her, as calmly as I could despite the sudden and terrifying urge to slap her. "But don't you dare hit your brother. Don't you dare hit Sam."

"Don't hit your *favorite* you mean. Let. Me. GO!" She gave one last ferocious yank and I relinquished my grip on her, noting as I did so the bleached bloodless ring I'd left around her wrist as she staggered away from me and wiped her nose on the back of her sleeve. Her eyes were red from weeping and narrowed with hostility as she scooped up her backpack.

"Jenny—"

She tugged open the door to the stairs—"Go to Hell"—and slammed it behind her hard enough to rattle the windows.

I stared after her for a moment. So did Sam. Then we looked at each other.

"She was bleeding," my son told me in a tone that suggested that it was a secret, one on many levels he didn't understand, and therefore assumed was not good.

"What?"

"There was blood coming out. From..." Embarrassed, aware that he was revealing something that didn't make much sense to him, he swallowed and pointed down at the crotch of his corduroy pants. "From down there."

My skin went cold, even as my face warmed with embarrassment and shame. "Oh."

"They made fun of her on the bus," Sam said, and in the same breath added, "Do you want to watch TV with me?"

Upstairs, Jenny slammed the door to her room no less violently than she had the downstairs one. I listened to her footsteps, then the strained protestations of the springs as she tossed herself upon the bed.

"Sure," I told Sam. He sat beside me on the sofa and leaned his head against my arm.

On the TV screen, anime characters squared off against each other.

"Why are their eyes so big?" I asked, to escape a reality that had abruptly become just as hostile and confusing as the nightmare.

"I guess so they can see better," Sam explained. His voice thrummed through my arm. "Do people in Japan really have eyes that big?"

"No," I told him, and mustered a fragile smile. "They don't."

FIVE

"JESUS CHRIST, GILLIAN, you could have been a little more sensitive." Chris was livid, and stalked around the kitchen, yanking at his tie and rubbing at his chin. He had spent the last hour upstairs with our daughter, and I gathered it had not gone well.

"Yeah, I would have been if I'd known," I protested. "But I'm not psychic. All I could see was that something was bothering her and she was acting like a brat about it."

"Wouldn't you in her place?"

"Chris, I didn't *know* she'd had her period."

"Well you should have. It's your job to look out for these things. I mean, didn't you ever talk to her about this kind of stuff?"

"Of course I did, but it doesn't seem to have made much of a difference. Today she was all about you. Shut me out completely."

Chris stopped pacing, his cheeks flushed. "And why do you think that is?"

"How the hell should I know? Maybe because you coddle her so much she automatically assumes I'm the asshole of the house."

"Yeah, well sometimes I think maybe she's right."

It was a low blow and one I knew he didn't mean. Even outside of temper, my husband had always been a talk first, think later kind of guy. Indeed, regret softened some of the steel in his eyes a moment later. But the damage had been done, and given my exhaustion and much maligned moods, combined with the guilt at how I had treated Jenny, it was all the excuse I needed to let free some frustration of my own.

"Maybe if you were here more instead of going to The Copper Lounge after work every day for those whiskeys you think I don't know about with those dead-end losers you call your friends, you'd have been here to deal with it yourself."

"At least those 'losers'—who incidentally you know less than nothing about—have wives who are capable of more than just sitting around gobbling pills and sleeping all day." His laugh was completely devoid of mirth. "Oh, I try to understand. You're having nightmares. Fine. But if it's such a problem, then do something about it instead of whining and moping around and making me and the children suffer as a result."

He resumed pacing. "You want to know what I think? I think it suits you to be so fucking miserable all the time. That way you can wallow in self-pity maybe because you feel you're not getting enough sympathy from anyone else."

"That's bullshit."

"It is? Really? Well maybe we've had enough of putting up with you acting like a ghost around here, Gillian. One of us has to work, and right now that's me. How am I supposed to do that if I know the kids aren't being looked after?"

He stopped right in front of where I sat at the table with my hands balled into fists.

"You dropped the ball today, honey. Big time. Jenny and Sam need you. I need you. And I just don't think it's fair that we should have to keep paying the price for something your father did to you twenty years ag—"

Teeth bared, I got up off the chair, my face inches away from his. Startled, he staggered back a step.

"And what the *fuck* would you know about any of that other than what I've chosen to tell you, huh? Not a goddamn thing. I don't talk to you about it because forced empty sympathy is exactly what I don't want and about all you'd be capable of."

He raised his hands in a placating gesture and turned his face away, grimacing as if it was my breath and not the words they carried he found offensive.

"We didn't all have perfect picket-fence *Home & Garden* childhoods, Chris. Sorry that you feel so fucking put out by that, or by the fact that I'm currently not perceptive enough to read our children's minds to save you from having to get your hands dirty."

"Okay, I'm sorry," he said quietly, and not entirely sincerely. "I'm sorry. I shouldn't have said that, but Jesus, calm down."

"Yeah, sure you're sorry, you fucking pious prick. To you, normality is when I'm handling everything and your role is relegated to undermining my laws and vilifying me so you come out the hero, but when you're called upon to actually *act* like a parent, it's an inconvenience to you. And one that has to be blamed on someone. So why not me, right? The weak one. Well fuck *you*." On the last word, I grabbed a steak knife from the table and flung it the length of the room. It struck the arm of a rocking chair, chipping the wood, and clattered to the floor. That chair, and the matching ottoman, had been a wedding present to us from Chris's mother. The sentimental attachment he felt toward that ugly piece of furniture was as strong as an umbilicus, and I'd just scored it with a knife.

I put my palms on the table and closed my eyes. A vein in my throat pulsed. I heard a clicking in my ears and realized I was grinding my teeth. Through them passed the words: "It wasn't my fault."

I wasn't quite sure to which incident I referred.

"Nothing ever is," Chris mumbled as he walked away.

"What?" I yelled, though I'd heard him perfectly. "What did you say?"

But he was already gone, headed upstairs no doubt to commiserate with our daughter on what a terrible mother I was.

When I noticed Sam's wide, frightened eyes watching me from over the coffee table in the living room, his face pallid and drawn in the blue-white glow from the muted television, I was no longer convinced they weren't right.

SIX

I AWOKE WITH A START TO A VOICE calling my name. It took me a moment to realize where I was. In the living room, which was dark but for the glow from the TV. Sam was curled up on my lap, snoring, his head against my breast. I raised my head. My mouth tasted rank from the three cups of coffee I'd had while trying to downplay the argument to Sam, who'd chosen to feign understanding as long as I agreed to watch *The Grim Adventures of Billy & Mandy* with him.

"S'ok," he'd said, with a tilt of his head. "I know you don't mean it. Daddy either."

He'd acted like all this adult stuff was beyond caring about, but I knew as well as anyone the potential psychological repercussions the behavior of adults can have on children.

My name again: "Gillian." Sharp and irritated.

Chris was at the door in a T-shirt and boxer shorts. His eyes were puffy from sleep, his face drawn and tired.

I blinked, dug sleep from the corner of my eye. "What?" I asked in a raspy whisper.

"It's midnight. Put Sam to bed."

I looked down at the top of my boy's head, as if to reassure myself that I hadn't simply dreamt he was there in a day characterized by estrangement from the ones I loved, and nodded. "Okay."

He disappeared, plodded upstairs. Nothing else to say. He wasn't one to let an argument die easily. Nor was I, for that matter, which made for some interesting and ugly periods over the course of our marriage.

I sighed and gently shook Sam. "Hey kiddo. Wake up."

He moaned, stirred only slightly.

"Sam." I shook him a little harder. "Time for bed." A little harder still.

And still he didn't wake.

"Sammy, you have to—"

He moaned louder then, as if in a nightmare of his own, and the fear in that sound hit me so hard I quickly adjusted myself in the seat, and he finally woke.

There was a look of pleading in his eyes.

There was something odd about his face.

"Sam?"

His mouth opened, kept opening wider and wider. Then I heard the sharp sound of a peanut shell being cracked as his jaw broke and muscles snapped to accommodate the width of his agony.

Oh Jesus...

Above his slack jaw, his small pink tongue worked madly, wordlessly, until it freed itself completely and tumbled from his mouth, landing to splat against my wrist.

My child began to convulse.

I tried to rise, but suddenly his small body had trebled in weight, perhaps filled with the shadows of the dream in which he had been imprisoned, as he brought his little arms up to embrace me.

I screamed hoarsely for my husband.

"Mom-mee?" Sam gurgled hollowly as dark blood spurted from his mouth.

I cried out in horror and felt the world tilt crazily away from me.

My baby's hands were gone.

In their place were the rusted hooks of a pair of clothes hangers.

SEVEN

I STOOD IN THE DRIVEWAY and watched as Chris stowed the bags into the back of the Toyota.

Sam was in the back seat, sleeping, worn out after a long night. Beside him, Jenny was listening to her iPod and staring down at her hands.

Ordinarily I would have considered it a beautiful day. We were edging out of summer into fall, and the leaves had already started to change. But that golden light blinded my tired eyes, and I had to force myself not to squint. Add in the fact that my husband was removing himself and the kids because, apparently, I was losing my mind, and the quality of the day was the last thing on my mind.

Chris wasn't leaving me. Not for good, at least, though I suspected unless something changed, we were going to look back on this as the start of it, the first volley in a war that was going to end badly. His mother would hardly be surprised, and I was bitter that it was from her he was going to seek solace. Once he got there, she'd treat him like a big child, and reinforce his misgivings about the woman he'd married. No doubt he'd tell her that I mutilated her chair. She hadn't liked me from day one. Why, was anyone's guess. Maybe because I wasn't the kind of woman she'd have chosen for him, wasn't like her. Or maybe because I was six dress sizes smaller than she. I could have told her that for all the years she'd been struggling with her weight, I'd been struggling to pull both mine and Chris's to keep the marriage afloat. Because she was a baby boomer, and more than happy to be walked on by her stevedore husband, Chris had been exposed to a decidedly uneven, and at times, chauvinistic view of how a partnership worked. I could have blamed her for that, for being a pushover, but what would that have gotten me only more discord from both of them?

Chris slammed the trunk shut, harder than was necessary, an unspoken protest at the way things had gone, or more accurately, the way I'd forced them to go.

"You know the number," he said. "We're going to King's Island first. Should probably arrive at Mom's by early evening." He opened the car door and added, without looking at me, "See you Sunday night."

"Okay."

He hesitated, as if there was something else he wanted to say. Maybe he wanted to ask why I wasn't blubbering or begging him to stay. A fair question, and one I'd have had trouble answering, if only because I'm not, nor have I ever been, a particularly convincing liar.

In truth, I wanted them to go. Just for a little while.

"Have fun," I told him. He looked at me as if that was a ridiculous statement, then nodded curtly and got into the car.

Anything that needed to be said he'd already taken care of the night I'd scared poor Sam almost to death. At the sound of my screams, Chris had come running down the stairs, the door flying open hard enough to slam against the wall, and before I knew what was happening, he had gathered Sam up into his arms and was hushing his tears, his eyes blazing as he looked at me. *What the hell is wrong with you?* I remember being confused, wondering why he was not as horrified as I was by our child's grotesque injuries. But then I'd realized the only thing wrong with Sam's face was that it was contorted by fear and sodden with tears. I'd been dreaming.

Chris had lectured me long into the night, and I'd said nothing. I hadn't needed his hostility to compound the guilt I felt, nor had I shared with him what I'd imagined had happened to Sam.

It would only have forced him to add further concerns about my mental stability to his already unflattering portrait of my relationship with my children.

The following morning, he had coldly informed me of his intent to leave.

"We could all use the break," he'd said. Meaning *they* could use the break from *me*.

I thought maybe I could use the break too, and that was part of the reason I hadn't argued with him, though he seemed surprised by my silence. "In the meantime, you might reconsider talking to someone."

"I will."

"Before you have nobody *left* to talk to."

EIGHT

I DREAM.

I am walking in darkness, my legs brushing against hard, unyielding wood that smells of lemon-scented furniture polish and ironically, of dust. Pews. I am inside the church, my footsteps echoing loudly, rising up to an arched ceiling I can see only in memory. It is the only sound in the world until I speak, my voice brittle and small. "Hello?"

I am alone, it seems, though there is the undeniable sensation of being watched.

I stop walking, if only to silence the maddening sound of my passage in the immense nothingness. It announces me, makes me a target. My hand finds the angled edge of a pew. The wood feels like cold skin, needled with course hairs that bristle to the touch. I recoil, and a light comes on, its source a figure sitting on the steps leading to the now-illuminated altar up ahead. It is my brother, John, sitting with his knees drawn up, his bare arms looped around them. I have seen him this way a thousand times. Even the mournful expression is familiar.

"John," I say, relieved, not only that he is here, but that he is whole again.

Behind the altar, just outside the reach of the glow that emanates from my brother, is a figure nailed to a cross. Such effigies are hardly uncommon in places such as these, but this one is. The figure is not of Our Lord, but one of his "brides", a woman wearing a nun's outfit—or a "penguin suit" as we used to call it back in the day. She has been crucified, rusty orange ingots driven through her feet and wrists. I cannot tell if there is a beatific expression on her face, because although her body is facing forward, her head has been turned around to face the wall upon which the cross is mounted. In the space in the wimple where her face should be, I see a fall of dark hair that reaches to her belly.

There is no way to identify who the woman is, but still I know, as I am meant to.

"Honey..." she whispers, the words muted by the proximity of her lips to the wood of the cross, "Forgive me..."

"Gillian," John says, regarding me from the steps, his features marred by a confusion of shadows courtesy of a spotlight from no discernible source. "This has to end. It's killing you."

"What is?"

"You know what."

"I don't."

"Don't be a fucking idiot, sis. You know what happened, what's still happening."

I am rendered paralyzed by the alien rage in his voice. It sounds like it belongs to someone far older than John, perhaps his adult self, had he lived to become it.

On the cross, my mother whimpers.

"You're broken," John says. "Badly. And it's going to cost you everything before it's over. I think you know this."

My voice, when I speak, is older now too, the voice of my real self, as if I have stepped fully into the dream. "I can't lose anything else, John. How do I stop it?"

"He can't touch you out there, so he chases you here, and you let him. But you're not running from him, you're running from yourself. He's not even real."

"What will happen if he catches me?"

He shrugs, even has the audacity to yawn, as if he's merely reciting lines. "Nothing of any consequence. It's the chase that matters, not the interception."

"So, it's just a ritual, like us rolling down the hill."

"Kinda. Except our ritual meant something, didn't it?"

I smile. "Yes. So much."

"That's why you're here. That's why you dream. We created a ritual to escape. It might have continued to work for you if I hadn't died. That poisoned the world we invented between us." He shrugs. "Sorry about that."

"I wish you hadn't died. I wish you were still alive."

"So do I."

"Really?"

He grins. "Nope. You're imagining me, sis. I'm only saying what you expect me to say."

"Well, I still wish you were with me. All of this would be so much easier to bear."

"Maybe, maybe not. Maybe you wouldn't even be talking to me. Maybe we'd hate each other."

"That's ridiculous. I love you."

"Hmm...see, that's the problem right there."

"What is?"

"Love. Do you think you're even capable of that?"

"Of course." But another voice, one I don't recognize or want to hear, pipes up from somewhere deep in the darkness inside me. *Do you, Jill? How could someone who has gone through what you have possibly know how to love? Wasn't that the price of surviving it all?* "I love you. I love my husband and my children with all my heart. How could I not? I've spent my life trying so desperately hard to treat them better than I, than *we*, were ever treated, caring for them more than anyone ever cared for us. Trying to make them happy."

"And are they happy?" John asks. "Is Chris happy? Are you?"

"Maybe not as much as they could be right now but that will change in time."

"He hurt me, Jill," John says. "Bad. Did he hurt you?"

"Yes. You know he did."

"Why?"

"I don't know. He said he loved us."

"Do you think he did?"

"I don't know that either."

"Maybe you should find out."

"How?"

"How else? Ask him."

Even in the dream, the idea is preposterous, and terrifying.

"He told me it was your time," John says.

"What does that mean?"

"He said you had finally become a woman, and he was excited to show you how much he really loved you. How much he was going to protect you from all the bad things in the world. But he was the bad thing, wasn't he?"

"Yes."

"Was I?"

I frown at that, try to discern his expression, but the light above renders his face little more than a white mask with dark holes for eyes. "Of course not," I tell him. I am sick, and suddenly desperate to wake, desperate to be gone from here, for though I have no sense of danger here, it feels as though something is coming.

"Were you?" John asks.

"No."

"Then why did you hurt me?"

"I didn't hurt you, John."

"Jack."

"Okay, Jack, I didn't hurt you. I loved you."

A faint gurgling sound that might have been my brother chuckling through a mouthful of blood. "Daddy said that too."

There is a sudden slam at the door behind me and even in the dream I am startled by the ferocity of the sound. The echo seems to linger in the air for far too long, until it is reinforced by another blow against the wood.

"Oops," John says. "Reality comes a-callin'."

"What do I do?"

"Sis, I have no answers for you that you don't already know, no conclusions you haven't already drawn. This is all your make-believe Hell, after all, and I'm just a figment of it. All I can say is what you want me to say, so here goes: If we were the nursery rhyme, if we were really Jack and Jill, how would it all end? I'd fall down, and break my crown..."

The light illuminating him extinguishes and now the dark is twice as dense as before. I am blind but for the afterimage of my brother and alone with the sound of the church door behind me being pummeled by the fists—or hooks—of a giant.

Wood splinters. Cracks.

My heart starts to pound.

Feeble gray light creeps through the gaps in the door. The hinges rattle.

"Hide," my mother whispers from the cross high on the wall.

But it is too late for that, and John's words are still ringing in my head with a fervor that mimics my father's assault on the door. A panel of wood separates with the sound of a gunshot and clatters to the floor. Now I can see the edge of my father's shoulder, a piece of the plastic wrapped around his head made foggy by his acrid breath.

I answer my brother's question. "...I'd come tumbling after."

The door explodes inwards.

NINE

"THE HELL DO *YOU* WANT?" the old man asked, and shut the door before I had time to formulate an answer. I stood on the stoop, chilled by more than the breeze, and stared at the chipped white paint on the front door. As I ran my finger over the tarnished brass number 9, I saw through the smoked glass panel that my father was still standing on the other side, back hunched slightly, head tilted as if listening. Slamming the door in my face had been a statement, a demonstration of his loathing. That he was lingering there meant curiosity had gotten the better of him. And who could blame him? It had been almost twenty years since we'd last seen each other. He had to be wondering what had brought me to his doorstep now.

"Open the door," I told him, struggling to keep the tremor from my voice, "Unless you want me to announce to the neighbors my reasons for coming here."

He did not hesitate long. We both knew the trouble neighbors could cause.

The man who yanked the door open had managed to age three decades in two and I guessed he'd probably grown even older still in the sixty seconds or so since he'd seen me on his stoop. His cheeks were sunken, the bones straining against the skin, pulling it taut. His face was angular, vulpine, the eyes bloodshot and all but lost in the folds of dark, wrinkled sockets. Broken capillaries formed a road map of regret across his nose. He had attempted to temper the mass of his silver hair with pomade, but something—

failing vision or poor lighting, perhaps—had caused him to miss frizzy clumps over his ears and the top of his skull. He wore battered work boots and a pair of denim dungarees over a red and white checkered shirt. From the opening, a tangle of wiry gray chest hair wound its chaotic way up to his wattled throat.

The odor he exuded was a noxious combination of sweat and alcohol.

He was exactly as I'd imagined he would be, as he should have been, though it was hard for me to reconcile the monstrous image I had carried with me since childhood with the wretched thing that stood before me now.

"The hell do you want coming around here?" he asked, warily.

"Can I come in?"

"For what? What do you want?" He did not move from the doorway.

"To talk."

"We have nothing to talk about."

"I think we do."

He shrugged. "I don't really care what you think or don't think. You've already caused me enough pain, so why don't you go back to whatever rock you crawled out from under and let me be." He started to close the door and I flattened a palm against it, stopping him.

"I'm not here to cause you trouble," I told him, unsure if that was the whole truth, and more than a little disgusted at the audacity of him playing the victim. "I just want...I need to talk to you."

He threw a cautious glance over my shoulder. The neighborhood was quiet, the street deserted.

The rain, which had been a mere drizzle to that point, quickly strengthened until it was hissing against the pavement.

"As soon as the rain goes away, you do too," he said gruffly, and turned away, leaving the open door as my invitation inside.

TEN

ENTERING THE GLOOMY HALLWAY was like stepping back inside the womb. Here was where everything began, and ended. Though the carpet in the hall had been changed in the intervening years, wasn't it here I knelt weeping, feeling the wooden floorboards pressing against my knees? To my right, the stairs, where I sat in the dark listening to my parents arguing about what to do with me, as if I was ever the problem?

The house was smaller than I remembered it, the rooms narrower, as if my absence had created a vacuum that pulled the walls in closer. The air smelled stale and dusty, rank with memory.

I followed my father into the living room. The light in here was dull, or perhaps the room had only possessed color in the old days, like a reversal of the photographic process. Boots scuffing against the carpet, the old man clicked the switch on a small shaded lamp. The yellow glow did little to add cheer, but illuminated enough to show just what had, and had not, changed.

"Sit down," he said, halfheartedly indicating a leather armchair that hadn't been there in my day.

The television was new. The sideboard was old and lined with pictures, some black and white (my father's parents, my parents' wedding), most faded color.

I noticed that there were no pictures of me or John in that gallery.

"Well?" my father said, brusquely. "Are you going to sit or what?"

Although loath to obey any command from him, I did, and took a moment to steady my nerves, to bolster the facade of false composure I'd had to maintain since leaving the car. I'd sat out there for an hour, watching the house, the breath sucked from my lungs at the sight of the place, struggling to summon the courage to come to the door, to do anything but turn tail and run, to take Chris's advice and just go see the damn shrink. Anything had to be better than this. After all, what was I doing but voluntarily going back into the lair of the monster, a monster I had for years feared I'd never escape?

But the dreams wouldn't stop, and my life was beginning to erode. I had to come here, to see if it might make a difference before everything was lost.

Still standing, he asked, "You want a drink or something?"

"I don't drink. Thank you."

"Surprising."

"Why is that surprising?"

"You come from a long line of drinkers."

And pedophiles? I almost asked, but figured if I wanted any kind of closure—assuming such a thing was even possible—it would be better to avoid antagonizing him, at least so soon.

"So...how long has it been? Fifteen years?" he asked.

"Something like that, yes."

"I suppose you're married now?"

"Yes."

"Kids?"

"Two."

He smiled bitterly. "Two grandkids and I didn't even know."

"You didn't know because they're nothing to you, and you're nothing to them. It didn't bother you to not know they existed, so let's keep it that way."

"Fair enough. Bit late to make any kind of a connection with them now anyway I suppose, assuming you'd even allow it."

"I wouldn't."

He smiled humorlessly. "Husband. Kids. Are you happy?"

"Do you care?"

He shrugged in response.

"Then let's cut the chit-chat."

"Fine." He cleared his throat. Since I'd arrived, the living room had become a source of renewed fascination for the old man. Anything to avoid making eye contact. "I assumed we were done with each other. Why the surprise visit?"

"I'm having trouble sleeping."

His bushy eyebrows rose. "And? Who doesn't? Why would that bring you here?"

"I'm having trouble sleeping," I explained, "because of nightmares. Memories of things that happened to me when I was a child."

Now he did meet my eye, and his stare radiated coldness. "And what do you think I can do about it?"

"You can answer a question for me. That's what you can do."

"About what?"

"You know what."

"I don't have any answers for you, missy. None that you'd care to hear anyway. I tried to talk to you when it mattered, when all the misery could have been avoided, back when we were buddies, you and me. Remember?"

My recollection of this was vague at best. What I could recall was my father with tears streaming down his face, eyes bulging with fear and anger and pain as he alternated between slapping and screaming at me: *Why? Why did you do this? I'm your father for fuck's sake! Do you* want *them to take me away?* And my mother, sitting in the kitchen, weeping silently, her flour-covered hands in her hair, fingers like glimpses of bare skull between the dark strands.

"Try again."

He sat down in a well-worn chair opposite me and sighed, rubbed a hand over his face. "Why are you really here?"

I closed my eyes for a moment and saw the faces of my family, the unit that had carried me this far through the battlefield of my own psyche. I saw Jenny, weeping; Sam, scared half to death; and Chris, with hurt and hate in his eyes as he loaded up the car. I imagined what it would feel like if their absence wasn't so temporary, if that departure had been the final one.

Then sweeter memories flashed behind my eyes.

I remembered making up excuses on my lunch break to visit the bank where Chris was a teller long before we knew each other. He'd worked just down the street from the library where I'd been employed since college.

I remembered the day he'd asked me out, our first date, the first kiss, the first time we'd made clumsy but sincere love in his apartment. The day he'd proposed.

I remembered all of this, and was reminded just how much things had changed. It was not too late for me to save my relationship with my children, but what about Chris? Had he already decided we were through? And if so, how badly did I want to fight to change his mind?

Perhaps I was wrong about how good a liar I was, and all along I'd been lying to myself.

I raised my head and looked at the old man sitting across from me. I hardly recognized him now, but I saw the awareness in his own eyes, the denial of guilt, the need to be a victim for fear of having to face again the darkness he'd allowed to consume him once upon a time. The darkness that consumed his children. The very same darkness that had touched me in my dreams all these years later and would consume my family if I let it.

"Why did you do it?" I asked him, anger burning like hot coals in my chest. "Why did you hurt us?"

My father seemed to sag, withdraw into himself as I watched, the result, I suppose, of having his estranged daughter, his *victim*, walk back into his life after a million years of enjoying conveniently rewritten history, only to have her throw the truth like ice-water right in his face. It gave me pleasure to see him affected this way.

"I never did anything to you."

"If you honestly believe that," I told him, "then I'm sorry for you. That you can sit there and lie to my face after what you put me through..."

"I never *hurt* you is what I'm saying," he protested.

"What's the difference?"

"There's a big difference in the eyes of the law. If you'd told them I was doting on you instead of *hurting* you, everything would have been different."

"But you *were* hurting me. Both of us. You were..." The words stuck in my throat. I realized I hadn't said aloud the things he did to me and John since that night Chris and I had sex for the first time. Even then it had been like trying to regurgitate barbed wire. Even then it had been the abridged version.

Stop, stop. Wait.

What's wrong? Did I hurt you?

At least Chris had had the decency to ask.

No, it's just...I need to tell you something...

"I'm a sick man, Gillian," my father said.

Don't I damn well know it.

"I've been ill for quite some time, and they've advised me to avoid stress. My heart..." He put a hand on his chest over the offending organ for dramatic effect. "It isn't so good anymore."

"And...what? I'm supposed to take pity on you?"

He looked almost sulkily at me. "No. I'm telling you why I can't talk about this anymore."

"Too fucking bad."

"Watch your mouth."

"Or what? Don't act like you're my father, *Jim*. It's a little too goddamn late for that."

"I want you to leave now. You ruined my life with this same crazy bullshit, and I only let you in because I hoped that maybe you'd finally come to your senses and realized what really happened, what I really did for you. I hoped we could try to fix the past, salvage something, but no, you're as stubborn as your brother was. Neither of you knew how to be loved."

I'd expected resistance, excuses, even pleas for forgiveness. What I hadn't expected was finding my father so utterly embroiled in delusion that he genuinely seemed to believe he had done nothing wrong. And even though such an attitude seemed perfectly suited to the monster that had chased me in my dreams for the better part of my life, I found myself appalled and stunned into silence seeing it here.

"Now, please Gillian," he said, rising from his chair, hand still clamped on his chest, "I'm asking you to leave...before I have to call someone."

"And who would you call?" The temporary paralysis his words had inspired melted quickly under the heat of renewed anger. "Mom? Can't do that. She's buried in wormy earth, driven there by a cancer I'm sure came about as punishment for a lifetime of looking the other way while you raped your children."

His face crinkled in disgust. "You're a vulgar bitch, you know that? How dare you come into my house and say such things. Haven't you caused enough trouble? We could have been a family. I loved you. I loved your brother, and look what you did. You took something special and you perverted it, made it ugly. Now get out of here, Gillian. Get the hell out of my house."

I stood too, my body positively thrumming now. "Or what?"

"I'm an old man. Old and tired and sick. I was a good father to you. You just didn't know how to be loved, and you made me regret ever trying. I won't try again."

"Love? Molesting children is not love, it's hate, no matter what way you try to justify it in that sick fucking head of yours. And how exactly have you paid for trying? Eight years of a twenty-five-year sentence? Then what? You've been sitting here in the safety of isolation, able to convince yourself that you never did anything wrong, never having to face me and answer for what you did. Never calling to ask my forgiveness. I bet you never bother to visit John's grave either, do you? No, because I guess it would be too much effort for you to beg forgiveness from a child you don't even have to look in the eye."

My father's face was slack and pale. Standing less than three feet from him, I knew that if I swung a fist, I could hit him, knock that look of self-pity off his withered old face, smash the teeth that smiled at me while he ran his rough hand up my inner thigh, shred the tongue that whispered false promises and veiled threats, blind the eyes that peered at me through lids hooded by arousal. I could have ended it right there and then, and though I wasn't sure if it was something of which I was capable, I was aware on some level that things had changed over the past few months. My chemistry, perhaps, as the experts would say. My wiring. In layman's terms, the things that made me tick had been altered and not yet tested. Because every time I woke from the dream, it was without a piece of my restraint. I had felt it around my own family, felt my control weaken around Jenny and Chris. If I lost it completely, better it be with the man responsible for it all than with them.

The old man's breathing grew heavy. His skin was almost gray.

"Why aren't you saying anything?" I asked him. "It's your turn, your *time* to say something. You've had long enough to be quiet." I was shouting, and knew it was inadvisable if I didn't want to draw unwanted attention. Those neighbors, of whom I thought fondly—particularly Mrs. Farris next door (though I had no idea if she still lived there), my savior when the time for running came—would have learned to regard my father's house as an ugly, loathsome place. They would have kept their children well away, gossiped amongst each other, and taken to advising new residents of where exactly the registered sex offender lived.

"I have to get my pills," my father said, and for the first time, I wondered if perhaps he hadn't been faking the severity of his ailment after all. He headed for the door.

"Get your pills then," I said icily. "But we're not done here. Not yet."

"We should be," he replied. "We have nothing more to say to one another."

"There's plenty to say if you just had the guts to say it."

Pausing only to give me an exasperated look, he eased himself out into the hall, leaving me alone with the sounds of the rain hammering on the roof and my pulse pounding in my ears.

As I listened to my father's slow passage up the stairs, each step punctuated by a grunt of effort, pity tried to dilute the anger and to a degree succeeded, but couldn't hope to water down the hate I felt for the old man. He was mentally ill, deluded, his words were testament to that, and I guessed him too far gone to be cured of it. Besides, to be cured, you must accept that there's a problem, and he believed no such thing. In his mind, he'd loved his children dearly, perhaps too much, and they'd turned on him as a result.

Twenty minutes passed. It was quiet upstairs. I wondered if he'd died up there, and envisioned him lying on the floor, skin white, lips blue, eyes bulging from their sockets, and I felt an alien and unwelcome pang of dismay. I justified the feeling by telling myself it was because no one wants to see a dead body, or to be burdened with the task of calling the necessary authorities and waiting around for it to be removed. But that wasn't the whole truth, and in this, it would seem my father was not the only one capable of creating alternate realities in which certain truths were omitted.

Reluctantly, I had to acknowledge the fact that, while I did not know what might have precipitated the change in him, nevertheless for a time, he was a good father, a normal father whose children had had no cause to question the purity of his love.

Once upon a time, Jack and Jill had a Dad.

An abrupt ache in my bladder, courtesy of the bottle of water I'd chugged on the way here, incited a ridiculous inner debate on what using the bathroom might signify to my father. I needed to go, but it seemed ill-advised to do so here, for fear that even something as simple as the need to use the toilet might be interpreted as a momentary dependency on him. *For decades you've had no use for me*, I imagined him thinking, *but you have use for me now, for I am KEEPER OF THE FACILITIES!* I sniggered quietly to myself. What a crock of shit. I was being absurd. But at least it had stopped me thinking about the good old days, which would have done nothing but lessen my resolve.

I looked up at the ceiling. A moment later, I heard him shuffling around up there. I did not sigh with relief, but felt it, and hated myself for even momentarily entertaining anything other than hostility toward him.

Perhaps he was hiding up there, afraid to come back down.

Perhaps he was searching for a weapon.

Jesus, get a hold of yourself. I was wasting my time, but at least I had confronted him, said aloud to his face the words that had been tattooed on my soul for longer than I could remember. That would have to suffice, and, I hoped, might make some little bit of difference to the turmoil that had my subconscious cocooned. From here, I had no recourse but to permanently erase him from my life, and now that I knew he was lost to his own lies and therefore incapable of change or remorse or salvation, it would be that much easier.

I shook my head, took one last look around the room, which not only looked much smaller now, but sadder too. There was a film of dust over everything as if it had resigned itself to being permanently forgotten and believed it should look the part. I had no connection to this place anymore, or anything in it. It had never been a home, just a stage where people acted their parts until the curtain was forced to close.

"I'm leaving," I called out, and made my way to the bathroom.

ELEVEN

THE FIRST THING I NOTICED was the smell of urine. The toilet hadn't been flushed and the water was a dark, unhealthy amber color beneath a ring of rust-colored grime. Specks of fecal matter clung to the back wall of the bowl. Empty toilet roll wrappers, cardboard tubes and used tissues overflowed from the small white plastic wastebasket to the left of the water tank. Sports magazines were scattered about the floor. They looked like they'd been there quite a while.

As I gently closed the door behind me, I caught a glimpse of myself in the water-stained mirror above the sink, which was veined with gray hairs and spotted with dark green buttons of hardened toothpaste. The woman staring back at me looked old and haggard, eyes beady, face an unhealthy pallor and framed by lank black hair. The repulsion on my face at the smell and the condition of the bathroom made me look ugly, witch-like. I was wearing the same jeans and blouse I'd worn the previous day, which made any harsh judgment of my father's slovenliness seem ironic. Luckily, I resemble my mother, which has kept me from seeing him in my reflection all these years or I'd most likely have been unable to live in a house with reflective surfaces.

I flushed the toilet and tugged free some lengths of toilet paper, which I placed around the seat as a makeshift barrier against whatever filth might linger there, then shucked down my jeans and sat. Even through the paper, the wooden toilet seat was cold, bringing a shudder and gooseflesh to my skin.

The only light in the room came from the stained, naked bulb built into the molding above the mirror and the small rectangular window over the bathtub to my right. The daylight was fading.

As I sat there, shivering slightly and listening to the inordinately loud sound of my pee hitting the water, I noticed something that hadn't registered on the way in. Directly in front of me, too far to reach out and touch from where I sat, was the door. When I'd lived here, that door had been solid wood, but sometime since, it had been replaced with one that had a glass panel inset in the top. That alone, would not have been enough to trouble me.

What did, so much so that I froze, my pee stopping painfully mid-flow, was that through that glass I could see the head and shoulders of someone standing outside the door, a shadowy figure, hands cupped around the face that was pressed against the warped glass. Peeking.

"What the hell are you doing? I'm *in* here!" I yelled, hoping that of the many emotions evident in that exhortation, it was the outrage not the fear that reached the voyeur.

With a sound of crinkling plastic, the face pressed closer to the glass and my bladder lost its previous reservations. For the moment, I was stranded on the seat, and willed the stream to hurry.

"I said there's someone *in* here." I was alarmed at the fear in my voice; it belied the forced confidence I had managed to maintain thus far.

The figure at the door did not move away, but turned its face to the side as if listening. Again, the crinkling sound, as of a freezer bag being crumpled.

Nothing about this made sense. It had to be my father out there, but the idea that he was deliberately trying to frighten me by dressing in the costume he wore in my nightmares didn't hold water. For one, I'd given him no details about the nightmare. For another, I hadn't heard him descend the stairs. Even forgetting those irrefutable facts, what could he possibly hope to gain by dressing as the very creature I had accused him of being?

I finish peeing and eschewed patting myself dry or washing my hands in favor of yanking up my pants and hurrying to the door. As I fastened the button on my jeans, his voice stopped me cold.

"*Open the door, baby...I want to see...*"

My throat went dry. After a moment spared to question the wisdom of what I was going to do, I flipped the lock on the door, grabbed the handle and yanked it open. *No more running*, I told myself, teeth clenched so hard they made my jaws ache. *No more fear. This ends now, and he's given me the perfect opening to hit him, hurt him, put him down for good.*

But there was no one there. I found myself looking, not upon my father in his pathetic nightmare costume, but across an empty hall at the closet door under the stairs, a sanctuary once upon a time. There was not a sound but for the rain.

Furious, I stalked down the hall and into the living room, my mouth already open and flooding with invectives.

The living room was empty.

How could he have hidden so fast? My father was old, so unless he'd stashed himself in the closet in record time, there was no way he could have moved away from the door without me seeing him.

A quick check of the closet revealed nothing but old coats, umbrellas, muddy boots, and an old vacuum cleaner.

Confused, I made my way upstairs, every step creaking beneath my feet.

Up here the atmosphere changed from one of neglect to sadness. There were three doors in this hallway, all but one of them closed. The first was my bedroom, and here I stopped. On the wood surface of the door I could still see the adhesive residue where once had hung a yellow vinyl sign that read: STOP: NO BOYS ALLOWED, a simple, innocent message, but one that might have altered the course of my life had it been heeded. My hand found the door knob, and there it lingered. What was there to be seen beyond this door? Had bitterness led my father to strip it bare, or had sick love forced him to preserve it? And what further impact did I think seeing the room would have on me, no matter what its state? Nothing would change if I looked; even less would change if I didn't. At length, I removed my hand, content to let the question go unanswered.

The next room was John's, and this door I did open.

It was almost as it had been the day he'd died. As in the rest of the house, the colors had faded, and dust covered everything, but his bed, a mattress nestled in a red racing car frame, was still there, as were his toys. Posters of *Transformers*, *Spider-Man*, and *The Incredible Hulk* covered the walls. I recalled a lot of fun times spent in here, helping John with homework, reading, or engaging in the ultimate standoff between my Barbie Dolls and his G.I. Joes, the battles made fairer by the mutually agreed upon stipulation that Barbie be armed with some of the military man's cache. Thus, it was not unusual to have Barbie doing a stiff-legged victory dance while G.I. Joe lay spread-eagled on the floor after being blown to bits by a grenade she'd kept stashed down her panties.

Of course, I remembered the bad times too, for it was not possible to allow one without the other following close behind. And so, I saw myself holding John as he wept, neither of us speaking, afraid to say the words aloud, to ask questions we knew no one our age could possibly answer, foremost among them always: *Why?*

As I did not yet have an answer to give my brother's ghost, I closed the door and moved on.

My father's door was open, and he was there, sitting on the bed. No costume, no plastic bag, no lascivious leer. He was dressed just as he'd been when he'd admitted me into the house, and he was crying.

He ignored my presence at the door, his attention fixed on the picture he held in his hands. It was a portrait of my mother.

"They don't understand," he moaned, stroking the picture with a tender forefinger. "Nobody does. You did though. I know you did."

Face contorted with grief, he sobbed uncontrollably and rocked slightly on the bed.

You imagined it, I realized. *The figure at the door. Just like you imagined what happened to Sammy.*

The pathetic creature on the bed was no longer capable of tormenting me, nor had he any desire to do anything but wallow in self-pity. *So here,* I decided, *I will leave him.*

But in doing so, I was finally admitting an elusive truth about myself: If I was still seeing things, projections from the nightmare, then the problem was not solely to be found with the old man on the bed before me, nor was he the solution. His transgressions had merely been the catalyst for a larger problem.

Something else was broken.

Quietly I made my way downstairs, and though I'm not sure what motivated me to do it—perhaps some stubborn belief that my father might still someday see his way to the light—I scribbled my phone number down on a piece of old notepaper and set it on his chair in the living room.

Then I left, with no answers, and no illusions or expectations that I would ever get a call from my childhood home.

But I did.

TWELVE

CHRIS AND THE KIDS ARRIVED HOME just after sundown on Sunday night, the day after I went to see my father.

There was a chill in the air that persuaded me to light the woodstove for the first time since the spring, and the house was warm, almost swelteringly so, something Chris guardedly commented on when he entered.

"Jesus, it's like a sauna in here." His face retained the same uncertain look laced with anger he'd left with, and I knew it would persist until I either proved that things had gotten marginally better since he'd left, or assured him his point had been made and taken on board.

"Temperature's supposed to drop to forty by midnight," I said, though I had heard nothing of the kind. I was cold; I lit the stove. No great mystery.

Jenny entered behind him, head bowed, attention fixed on her cell phone, a gift from her doting father I had vehemently protested. "Hi Mom," she mumbled.

"Hey honey. How was your trip?"

"Okay, I guess." She continued through the living room, and up the stairs.

"She had a little falling out with Grandma," Chris said. "About the amount of time our daughter spends on that phone."

"For once, I think I'm on your Mom's side," I said. "If we don't do something, Jenny's going to lose the ability to raise her head. People will have to kneel down to talk to her."

Chris grinned. "Joke all you want, but there's nothing more intimidating for a guy than being in a room with two pissed-off women."

I shrugged. "So it was no better up there than it was here, huh?"

His grin faded. He looked down at the car keys in his hands. "You know how she can get."

"Intimately familiar."

"So...how was your weekend? The quiet do you any good?"

"Didn't catch up on sleep, if that's what you're asking. And the nightmares haven't stopped."

"Didn't think so. Did you at least have a chance to—?"

He was interrupted then as Sam barreled in the door, arms spread wide for a hug for which I hardly had time to prepare before he slammed into my legs and embraced my knees instead. "MOMMY!"

"Hey baby! Did you have fun at Grandma's?" I reached down and pried him loose, then hoisted him up into my arms.

He nodded. "Uh-huh. Are you and Daddy getting divorced?"

And right there I had the full story about what my husband and his mother had discussed. I had expected as much, but it still stung to hear it, and it annoyed me that they'd been careless enough to have had such a conversation within earshot of Sam, if not Jenny too.

I gave Chris a sour look, then reignited my smile for Sam's benefit. "Don't be silly, kiddo. Nobody's getting a divorce."

"Sure?"

I nodded. "Cross my heart."

"Okay. Did you get sleep?"

"A little," I replied, touched by his concern, but aware that he was probably only asking because it was another subject that had been broached at his grandmother's. "Thank you, honey."

"Uh-huh," he said, and wriggled to be set free. I set him down. "Can I watch TV? Grandma wouldn't let me watch Cartoon Network at her house."

"Why not?"

"Dunno. She said it was in...inaportimate."

"Inappropriate?"

"I guess."

"Well, no such rules here," I said. "You go right ahead and watch whatever you want."

"Yay!" he cheered. He raced into the living room and dove onto the couch, sending cushions flying.

"Half an hour, bud," Chris called to him. "Then bedtime. You've had a long day today."

"Awwww," Sam moaned, more because it was his duty as a child to do so, rather than out of any real regret. Then the TV bloomed to life and his expression softened as he forgot what it was he was supposed to be disappointed about.

I looked at Chris. "Real bitching session, huh? And in front of the kids. Nice."

"It wasn't like that," he said, irritated. "Jenny asked me if we were getting a divorce, and Sam was there. I guess one of her friend's parents just filed a separation agreement, and the kids have been talking. It's natural for them to be concerned when they see us arguing as much as we have been."

I nodded, and leaned back against the kitchen counter. I wasn't sure if that was the whole truth or not. After all, it would hardly be a staggering change of form for his mother to badmouth me, but I let it go. Besides, after visiting my father I had decided that it was time to start working on fixing things rather than contributing further to their decay. The nightmares weren't going away, but if I didn't do something fast, my family would. And they were all I had left.

"Guess we'll have to work on that then, right?"

Chris stood about a foot away from me, a distance most couples would feel comfortable closing with a kiss, or at least an embrace. But even though it was fragile, the barrier between us was still there, so instead we just offered each other uncertain smiles.

"Right," he said, then exhaled heavily. "I'd better unload the car." He called to Sam, "Hey lazybones, thanks for helping me with the bags!"

"Welcome," Sam called back, without looking away from his cartoon.

Chris rolled his eyes at me. "He gets that from you, y'know."

"You wish." I smiled after him, filled, however briefly, with the hope that maybe, just maybe, there was a chance here.

At the door, he stopped, started to say something, then shook his head.

"What?" I asked.

He stood on the threshold, looking thoughtful. Behind him, the last of the day's light was dying. "It's stupid. Never mind."

I sighed. "If it was stupid, then you shouldn't have made a production out of it because now I *want* to know, dummy."

He appraised me for a moment, and in his eyes, instead of the anger and frustration I'd grown accustomed to seeing of late, I saw the same dim light of hope I felt inside myself, the desperate need to keep things from slipping away.

"I was going to ask if you wanted to go out later," he said, and shrugged, as if to say: *told you it was stupid.* "After the day I've had, I could use a taste."

"Go out where?"

"I don't know. We could hit a bar in town. O' Reilly's maybe. Like we used to. Bit of nostalgia."

"We don't have a sitter."

He waved away the thought. "It'd only be for a couple of hours, and Jenny's old enough to keep an ear open for Sam."

I scoffed. "Whenever her ears aren't plugged with her iPod, you mean. And the stove's lit. She wouldn't know what to do if it started acting up."

"Acting up, how?"

"I don't know...if the pipe overheated or something."

He started to turn away. "Forget it."

"Wait." I touched his arm, halting him. He looked from my face to my hand on his arm, which made me wonder when I had last touched him in any significant way. *Christ, I thought, you've been mired so deep in your own misery you haven't even realized he's sharing it.* "Okay."

A smile began to curl his lips. "Okay?"

"Yeah. But you talk to Jenny. Tell her not to touch the stove. I'll turn it off before we leave. The place will stay plenty warm until we get back."

His smile was so heartbreakingly genuine my eyes grew moist at the sight of it. "I'll tell her."

I nodded. "Good. And bring your cell phone so she can contact us if she needs to."

"You got it."

"Give me half an hour or so to get cleaned up and we can head out."

"Okay." As I watched him hurry to the car for the bags, I thought, *Definitely a chance to save us.*

It helped that for the first time in months, I wanted to.

THIRTEEN

O' REILLY'S WAS ALMOST EMPTY but for the few world-weary souls seated around the bar who stared at us as we entered as if hoping we were salvation come to spirit them away. A trio of long-haired musicians were setting up instruments on the raised stage next to the entrance, and looked distinctly unenthusiastic to be doing so, though the lead singer, fifty years of age at least, with blond hair and a rugged face, carried himself with a swagger that suggested he'd once been successful and expected to be again.

"The usual?" Chris asked as we approached the bar.

"Sure."

He ordered a Heineken for himself, and, as I had sworn off alcohol (though recent events might have excused my prodigal return), an orange juice for me. The barman, a stocky fratboy type with a pudgy face and an OSU T-shirt, looked with something like sympathy at Chris as he handed over the latter beverage, as if to say, "Good luck gettin' any tonight, man."

Chris ignored him, paid for the drinks, and we made our way to a table as far from the band, and everyone else, as we could find.

"This place has gone to hell," Chris said with a rueful sigh as he settled himself down across from me. "Remember when we used to come here with Grace and Mike? It would be jammed on a Sunday night. Now, I don't know whether it's the economy or what, but...*Jesus*."

Grace and Mike Shields had been a couple who'd lived across the street in the new development opposite ours. Mike had been an attorney, Grace a real estate agent, and between them they'd made more in a year than we could in five. Social status and financial success notwithstanding, however, we'd become friends after they locked themselves out of their house one winter's eve and had to borrow Chris's ladder. Beer and wine had followed, became a weekly ritual, then a biweekly one, until we were practically living at their house. They had one child, Martin, who was autistic, but seemed to tolerate Sam's hyperactive attention cordially enough. The Shields seemed to have everything, but never lorded it over us, and I was glad to have a friend in Grace, who, once you dug down a little, wasn't nearly as together as she pretended. Neither, according to Chris, was Mike. They had simply committed to the image of perfection while missing many of the vital components necessary to make it work. Among those missing requirements was fidelity, and though each had suspected the other of cheating, it wasn't until Grace walked in on Mike in bed with his paralegal—a male paralegal—that she decided it was time to dissolve the pretense, and their marriage. Mike moved out shortly thereafter. Grace kept the house for another six months, but was rarely there, until finally it sold to a couple who apparently wanted nothing to do with their neighbors if it could be helped.

"I miss them," I said to Chris. "Good people."

"Good, but messed up," he said.

"True, but you could just as easily apply that description to us, right?"

He nodded somberly, took a sip of his beer.

I put my hand on his. "Hey, but we're far from done, right?"

His smile was not inspiring, and after a moment he said, "I just wonder what happened, you know? Fine, neither of us ended up where we hoped we'd be, but that happens to everyone, doesn't it?

"Sure it does. It's life's biggest joke. Allow you your dreams then slam the door in your face when you're halfway to realizing them."

"I just remember things being so much better. So much less...*work.*"

"Do you blame me?" I asked, and when his eyes met mine, I smiled reassuringly. "I'm asking honestly, and if you say 'yes' I won't freak out, I promise. I know I've been a lot of the problem, but do you think I'm all of it?"

"Of course not. What's happening with you has just made it harder, that's all. I hate seeing you this way, and when you won't let me help, I feel...useless."

"I know. I didn't for a long while, but I do now. Over the past few days, I've started seeing what's been happening to me through your eyes, and the kids' eyes, and I can't stand it. What you said the other morning, about me needing help, you were right."

He looked surprised. "Yeah?"

"Yeah. Tomorrow morning, I'm going to find a shrink and make an appointment."

Chris beamed. "That's great!"

"I'm not saying it'll help. I still think psychiatrists are crazier than their patients and about as competent, but I'll give it a shot. Baby steps, right?"

"Baby steps," Chris agreed, and toasted my glass with his bottle. "I'm proud of you. For trying, at least. And for the record, I don't think you're crazy. Just a little..."

"Bugshit?"

He laughed loudly. "Let's go with stressed. We'll wait for the shrink's verdict before we downgrade your diagnosis."

"Before you get too giddy, remember therapy isn't going to come cheap."

"What do you want to do? Sell one of the kids?" He grinned wryly.

"No, I already looked into that. Ohio isn't one of the states where it's allowed."

"So, what are our options?"

"We could tip some whale hunters to the location of your mom."

Chris rolled his eyes. "Jesus, Gillian."

"*Or*, I can call Dan and tell him I've been sick and ask if he'll let me come back to work on Wednesday."

Chris sighed, obviously pleased that the ice over my heart had thawed. And though that wasn't entirely true, not yet, I was committed to getting there, to restoring some semblance of order in the chaos our lives had become. When things had been good between us, they'd been very good. I wanted that again.

As the night went on, the band painfully demonstrated why success had eluded them, and patrons more selective than we entered, heard the band, and promptly reversed course while I measured the time in the amount of beer bottles that collected on the table. Though Chris had never been a bad drunk, nor did he seem to know when to stop. If the alcohol was there, he would keep drinking it until he passed out, threw up, or both. He claimed it was his Irish blood that gave him such a great tolerance for liquor. I preferred to think of it as a lack of discipline combined with immaturity and weak will. He also tended to get emotional, and after nine beers and a shot of 151, that night was no exception.

"I love you, baby," he said, his eyes glassy, lips downturned as if his proclamation had been an apology.

"I know you do, and you can tell me how much on the way to the car. It's after midnight. We told Jenny we'd be back by now. We need to get going."

He blew air out through his lips and waved a hand at me. "Home. Christ. It's early."

"Not for people with kids it isn't, and you have work tomorrow."

He shook his head in a way that reminded me of Sam. "I hate that fucking place."

"Home or work?"

"Work."

I smiled indulgently. "Since when?"

"Since always." He was starting to slur, and the words came out as *Sssince awlays*. "Ten years I'm there and I'm always the last to get any credit or recognition for anything. Fucking Kelvin Foley gets promoted twice and he's been there...what? Five years? Stubby little asshole."

"Good work always gets recognized eventually," I said, then jolted as the lead singer yowled into the microphone and adopted a rocker stance that looked like it was going to cause him a groin injury.

"You'd think so," Chris said, and began to pick at the soggy label on his beer bottle. "I don't know. I need a vacation. And a new job. Before I burn that fucking place down."

I couldn't help it, I laughed. He'd looked so sincere.

"Easy for you to laugh," he said. "Maybe I'll pull your stunt and call off for three weeks." He raised a hand. "No...no judgment, swear to God. Just saying. It'd be nice."

"Yeah, yeah. I have a feeling I'm going to be dealing with your not-so-subtle jabs for quite a while."

The band finished mangling Leadbelly's "Where Did You Sleep Last Night?", and graciously thanked the nonexistent audience for their nonexistent applause.

"I'd never," Chris said, and belched. The smell of stale beer rolled into my face, and I grimaced. "Sorry," he added.

I made a point of checking my watch. "Look Chris, if you're not done getting your drunk on, there's beer in the fridge at home, but we have to go."

"Will I have to share?"

"I don't drink, you clown, now come on." I slid off my chair and went to him. He raised his hands in surrender.

"What would I do without you?" he asked, rising unsteadily to join me.

"You'd probably have more hair," I told him.

"Ouch."

FOURTEEN

I DROVE, DESPITE CHRIS'S INSISTENCE that he was more than capable, and when we returned home the house was quiet and dark.

"Jesus," Chris said. "Leave a light on why don't you?"

"I told her if we were later than midnight to lock up and turn everything off," I explained.

"Very responsible of you, but potentially problematic for the vision-impaired drunkard."

"You're right. Next time I'll have her set a candle out for the souls of the recently inebriated." I squeezed his arm, then cracked open the door of the car. Instantly the night air rushed in to greet me, my breath forming clouds before my face.

"Hey," Chris said, as I was halfway out of the car.

"What?"

"We're gonna make it, right?"

"Inside?"

"You know what I mean. Be serious."

"Yeah, I know what you mean."

"Tell me honestly. No bullshit. We're going to make it. We are, right?"

I stared at him, the chill infecting me, and in that moment, I saw the depth of his pain. The alcohol did more than make an emotional jester out of him; it forced his guard down too. Sitting there with the dome light scalding his face with shadows, I knew without a doubt that I loved him, and that I was sorry for what I had put him through.

"We are," I said. "And if we don't, it won't be because we didn't try."

He nodded, and watched a moth trying frantically to get at the light from the other side of the windshield. "Good. Because as hard as things have been, I can't even imagine what my life would be like without you in it."

"You'll find out soon enough if you don't get me out of this cold, Chris."

"All right, all right," he said, opening his door and stepping out. "Christ, you say something nice and all you get in return is whining. Ladies and gentlemen, welcome to my world."

I waited for him to come around to my side of the car and looped my arm around his waist, ostensibly to support the drunken fool, but also because I just plain wanted to. We'd forgotten how to be intimate with each other, and as part of the healing process, I figured it was time to start remembering.

* * *

"I'm gonna use the little boy's room," Chris said, as we stepped inside. I closed the door behind me and quickly flipped on the light, just in time for him to realize he was headed straight into the kitchen counter. He stopped short, raising his hands and looking over his shoulder at me to see if I'd caught the near-collision.

"Good one," I said.

A sheepish grin and he rounded the counter, back on course to the bathroom.

On the small table in the sunroom, a red number 1 was pulsing in the phone's LED display, and while I listened to Chris's off-key whistling, I debated whether or not to check the message. I set my purse down on the table and decided it could wait. Checking on the kids was infinitely more important than what I suspected was either another telemarketer, ignoring the rules about appropriate times to call, or worse, Chris's mother. If the latter proved to be the case, then it would be just the thing to end the night on a bad note, and I wasn't willing to let that happen. Although I knew months of damage couldn't be undone in a few hours, tonight had certainly been an encouraging start. We would have to be careful around each other for a while, but if I stuck to the promises I'd made while maintaining a more positive attitude, regardless of whether the nightmares continued or not, it would prove to Chris that I was dedicated to rescuing us. He would have to play his part too, of course, but I had seen in him that he was willing, and for now, that was enough.

"I'm going to check on the kids," I called to Chris.

"Okay. Now that I've made room, I'm gonna have a beer. Just one."

"You're going to regret this in the morning."

"Oh, didn't I tell you?"

"Tell me what?"

"I have the day off tomorrow."

"Since when?"

"Since about a minute and a half ago when I walked into the sink and then tried to take a leak without taking my tire iron out of the trunk. Also, I have the distinct impression my esteemed and foul-smelling boss Mr. Taylor would rather not start his day watching me upchuck a half-dozen McDonald's hash browns into his wastebasket. So, humanitarian that I am, I'll spare him the ordeal."

"Sounds like you have it all planned out," I said.

"I think it's best for all concerned." He pronounced this *conzerned*.

Smiling, I made my way through the living room and headed upstairs.

* * *

I checked on Sam first and found him asleep in one of those positions unique to children of that age. He was lying on his stomach, face mashed into the pillow, mouth open, butt raised slightly in the air, knees bent, as if he'd dozed off while kneeling. He was drooling slightly—*his mother's son*, I thought wryly—and as always, he'd managed to kick the covers not only off himself, but off the bed too. They lay in a pile on the floor.

As I picked up the comforter, I looked around and was reminded of my brother's room. I felt a brief twinge of regret that I hadn't explored my own room when I'd had the chance, if only to compare how it had been treated by my father. I had the sad feeling I'd have found it either bare or used for storage. Sam's bedroom, like John's, had barely an inch of wall that was not covered in posters, though instead of cartoon and comic book superheroes like *The Hulk* and *Spider-Man*, my son preferred to gaze upon characters from video games. Here was a scowling Kurt Russell-looking figure dressed like a ninja. There was a handsome if ridiculously overbuilt guy wielding an equally oversized gun flanked by an exotic and buxom female sidekick as they pumped rounds into a horde of the undead. Yet another poster showed what was presumably a man, dressed from head to toe in a copper-colored and segmented spacesuit, his visor filled with blue light as he posed in the doorway of what I supposed was a spaceship of some kind. I vaguely recalled seeing Sam engrossed in these games, none of which I'd thought appropriate, all of which Chris had assured me were fine. Another battle I'd lost and one that didn't seem quite as monumental now as it had back then.

Sam never slept without his night-light on. He told us it was simply so he could find his way to the bathroom if he woke up in the middle of the night, but we knew better, and had no plans to dissuade the habit. He would outgrow it in his own time, and both Chris and I could clearly recall those nights when we were children when no amount of adult assurance could convince us there wasn't indeed something in the dark just waiting for us to be left alone.

In my case, that suspicion had been confirmed on many occasions.

I spread the comforter over my son and tucked the edges under the mattress. It wouldn't make a difference, I knew. He'd find a way to kick them off again, but he'd be warm for a while at least. As I bent down and kissed his brow, he mumbled "Mommy?" and I whispered to him a good night. He chewed contentedly on his dream and went back to sleep.

I slipped out of the room, hesitating briefly at the door to wonder how I could ever have doubted my devotion to this beautiful little boy, to my daughter or my husband, and shook my head.

You have a lot of work to do, lady, I thought, and gently closed the door.

* * *

Jenny had, only in the previous year, instituted a new rule regarding her privacy. If the door wasn't ajar, then we had to knock and wait for an answer before entering her room. We were informed that it was never okay to just walk in, nor did we have the right. And though we of course knew she was absolutely entitled to her privacy, and had expected such declarations of secession from our decidedly uncool dominion for quite some time, we had to marvel at the way in which her demands were conveyed. She made it clear that these were not requests, but rules, and to violate them meant suffering her wrath, which translated as a hissy-fit and silent treatment that could last for weeks. The problem with this rule, however, was that another recent change in Jenny's life had been her discovery of and subsequent dependency on music, ubiquitously carried to her ears via the iPod Chris had bought her the Christmas before, so that even when we knocked on our daughter's door, chances were she wouldn't hear us. This left only two options: knock louder, a tactic we could only employ when Sam wasn't asleep in the next room, or: enter the room anyway and just hope that Jenny wasn't indisposed, or otherwise engaged in something deemed unsuitable for parental consumption by her high school BFFs.

I knocked on the door and waited. No sound from inside the room, not even the faint tinny buzz of the music being pumped into her brain. I gave it thirty seconds or so and then knocked again, a little louder this time.

Another thirty seconds, and I eased open the door, just enough to increase the chances of Jenny hearing me, not enough for her to declare it an invasion, and called her name.

No answer.

From downstairs, I heard the clink of a bottle and the *whush* of the fridge door closing. Suddenly I was eager to be back down there with Chris, capitalizing on this ceasefire before he got too drunk or too maudlin, or both. *And*, I told myself, *you're the adult here for Chrissakes, yet you're standing outside your daughter's door like you're afraid of her.* I frowned. Respecting her wishes was one thing, but acting like she was the boss was granting her a little too much power for her age. If it led to a war, then fine, I was willing to fight it, but Jenny would have to understand that if she wanted her privacy respected, she'd have to be available to hear it when someone came to her room.

I pushed the door open. It was dark inside, but the expanding wedge of light from the hallway allowed me to see that Jenny was sitting at her desk in her nightdress, her back to me.

"Hey, didn't you hear me?" I asked.

Clearly, she hadn't, nor did it appear as if she'd heard me now. She just continued sitting there, motionless, so much so that I wondered if she'd fallen asleep in the chair.

"Jenny?"

Listening to that damn music, I thought, annoyed.

But then I glanced at her unmade bed and saw the iPod lying amid the folds of her comforter like a raft in the troughs of a rough sea.

I sighed—*nothing's ever easy*—and reached for the light switch. Jenny's voice, little more than a whisper, stopped the motion, and my heart, with four simple and yet devastating words: "He touches me, Mommy."

I did not look at her. Did not move. Instead I stared at my hand, frozen inches from the light switch, my shadow a misshapen lump thrown against my daughter's bedroom wall, and I told myself I had misheard.

At length, "What did you say?" I asked her, and whispered a short prayer, the first I could recall uttering in my adult life, that her response would be something benign.

What I got was no answer at all.

I waited, held in place by panic. "Honey," I asked the quiet room. "Honey, what did you say?"

Again, only silence.

"Jenny, answer me." How I longed in that moment for the familiar and ordinarily infuriating hornet-in-a-jar buzz from her iPod ear buds. It would have been a normal, innocuous, everyday sound in a room that suddenly felt pregnant with expectant dark.

Sick to my stomach, I jerked my hand upward and light flooded the room. I snapped my head around to Jenny, to the chair, and found it empty, my daughter's name dying on my tongue before I had a chance to speak it.

Confusion buzzed through me, the taste of copper filling my mouth as a new headache tapped gently but insistently at my right temple. Another hallucination?

I looked again toward the bed, at the folds where the iPod lay, and realized those folds had formed around my daughter's body. She was in her bed, and squinting up at me through newly wakened eyes. Her hair was spread out around the pillow, and she frowned at me and raised a hand to block the glare of the light.

I slowly, carefully sat down next to her, as if afraid she might prove intangible, another facet of my imaginings. "What did you...?" I began to ask again, then thought better of it. It was clear now that she had been in her bed all along. The covers were warm, the ear buds still nestled in her ears. She had fallen asleep while listening to her music. Nothing strange about that. Nothing strange here at all. And yet there was a lingering unease in my chest, an unsettling feeling in my brain that indeed something *was* wrong here, that I'd imagined nothing. Perhaps my exhaustion combined with the shadows in the room had merely composited an optical illusion from clothes, flattening perspectives of various objects to form an impression of my daughter's likeness sitting at her desk. It seemed unlikely given the clarity of what I'd seen, but fine, if I had to concede that it was possible, if not probable, then I could. But what of her words? Had I imagined them too? Or simply misinterpreted as sinister something she'd mumbled in her sleep? Maybe she'd been dreaming, and said: "Here to tuck me, Mommy?" and not "He touches me, Mommy." But she was too old for such infantile requests and I knew it.

I brushed a lock of my daughter's hair away from her forehead and she offered me a wan smile.

"You okay?" she asked.
"I am. You?"
"Uh-huh. What time is it?"
"Late. Go back to sleep. I'm sorry I woke you."

She nodded and closed her eyes.

I rose, and stood for a moment watching her. Then: "Jenny?"

"Mmm?"

"Thank you for watching Sam tonight."

"S'ok."

You saw nothing, I told myself. *You heard nothing. And if you did, remember what happened with Sam. You're tired, and sick. You need help. Until you get it, keep it together. It'll be fine in the end. Just hold on.*

I bent down and kissed Jenny on the forehead, just as I had done with Sam, the difference being that if Jenny had been fully conscious, she wouldn't have stood for such an overt display of affection. Likely, she'd have scowled and reminded me how old she was. But the kiss was less for her than for me. I needed the emotional contact to remind myself I was still here among people who loved me, and not on the far side of some dark plain screaming at hallucinations while the real world tried to shake me off. I was afraid, and no amount of self-counseling could lessen the feeling. If I was imagining all of these crazy, nightmarish things, how crazy did that make me? What if the therapist heard my story and decided the best thing for me was institutionalization or a pharmaceutical regimen that would turn me into a drooling zombie? *Would it be any worse an existence than this one?* I asked myself and decided that no, it wouldn't. I had agreed to try alternatives, and as it stood, any of them would be better than being unable to get through a day not populated by hallucinations and nightmares, or the expectation of same.

I turned off the light, and exited Jenny's room.

I did not look back.

Just in case she was there again, sitting at her chair, whispering.

FIFTEEN

WHEN I CAME DOWNSTAIRS, I found Chris sitting at the kitchen counter, a bottle of beer in one hand, a cigarette in the other.

"Smoking?" I asked him, with half-hearted disapproval. Once upon a time, we'd both shared the habit, but I'd quit on my thirty-first birthday, and Chris had followed suit six months later. Still, we kept a pack in a drawer in the garage just in case events conspired to make having one seem a good idea.

He shrugged. "Just felt like it. Got tired of talking to myself."

"Sorry about that." I poured myself a glass of orange juice, and as I rounded the counter to look upon him directly, I saw to my dismay that he'd been crying. *Looks like the window of good cheer has closed and the skies have turned gray again*, I thought. "What's the matter?"

"Not sure." He looked with fierce intensity at the cigarette clamped between the index and middle finger of his right hand. "I had a good night tonight."

"Me too."

He sighed shakily and took a drag on his cigarette, exhaled smoke. "Is it going to stay like this?"

"Like what?"

He gestured at himself, then me. "This."

"If we want it to, it will, sure."

"Good." He drained his beer. "That's good."

I noticed he wouldn't meet my eyes. "What's eating you?" I asked, suspecting that it was something other than just our present situation.

"Nothing," he said, frowning. "It's nothing." Then he did look at me, if only briefly, and gave me a tired smile. "I'm just drunk. You know me when I've had one too many."

"Or nine," I said.

"Yeah. Maybe I'll go to work tomorrow, after all."

"What made you change your mind?"

He stubbed out the cigarette in his bottle cap. "The money, I guess. Like you said, the shrink isn't gonna be cheap."

"True," I agreed. "But we'll figure it out. And it'll help when I'm back to work too."

He nodded, stood. "You staying up for a while?"

"I wasn't planning on it, no."

"Okay. Think I'm gonna turn in."

"I'll be there in a minute," I told him. "Make sure you brush your teeth and spritz yourself with some deodorant when you go up."

He gave me a quizzical smile. "Why?"

"If you don't, the kids will smell the beer and cigarettes on you when you kiss them goodnight." *And don't you clearly recall Daddy reeking of those very things?* a voice inside me whispered unkindly.

"Yeah, you're right." Chris looked disappointed. I knew why, but waited until he turned and started for the stairs before I alleviated that feeling for him. "And because I don't much like the taste of it myself."

He smiled, uncertainly at first, until I mirrored it.

"See you upstairs," he said.

* * *

"I'm sorry," Chris said later. He was sitting naked on the edge of the bed, lit only by the sulfuric glow from the streetlight outside our bedroom window. His face was a mask of blurred and jaundiced shadows. "I don't know—"

"It's all right," I said, releasing his flaccid cock after a good half hour spent trying in vain to get him hard. As I rose and tugged on my panties, he leaned forward and put his head in his hands.

"Fuck," he said with such ferocity that spittle speckled my bare belly.

I put my hands in his hair and hushed him. "It's not a big deal, Chris. You're drunk, and it's been a while."

He made a startling sound then, an odd strangled noise I had never heard from him in all our years of marriage. Alarmed, I tried to take a step back, but he wrapped his arms around my waist and pulled me closer, pressed his face hard against my stomach. In an instant, I felt dampness against my skin as he wept.

So many tears lately, I thought. *From everyone I know.*

"What's wrong?" I asked and stroked his hair. "Tell me."

"It hasn't been a while," he sobbed, and I felt his body convulse as it pumped wave after wave of tears out of him.

"What do you mean?" It was a redundant question, because although I had spent the last few months with a tenuous grip on my faculties, the one condition that could never be attributed to me was stupidity. And like the old sage sayeth: *A woman knows.*

It took him a long time to answer, and the delay only reinforced the certainty in me that I had been betrayed. His eventual response confirmed it.

"I've done something I'm not proud of, baby. And...I'm so fucking...sorry..." More tears, more convulsions followed. I continued to stroke his hair, aware that it might be interpreted as forgiveness, especially given his alcohol and guilt-induced vulnerability, but this was not a typical time in our relationship, and it seemed best, at least until better options presented themselves, not to shut him out. Instead, I allowed him the closeness, let him kiss my belly with his snot-slick lips like an underling seeking clemency, and stared down at the top of his head, at my fingers in the chestnut forest of his hair, and I waited.

"It wasn't planned," he said, voice thick with sorrow. "I swear to you it wasn't. It just happened."

Why? I wanted to ask, but didn't. I knew why, just as instinct had informed me of his deeds before he had. It made a certain sick sense that, given my recent behavior, my condition, a lonely man would seek solace and satisfaction in the arms of another woman, no doubt a more stable and loving one. The hate, which had never really retreated, had merely stepped out for a while until it was needed again, returned, like ink dropped into the water of my consciousness.

"It had been so long, and...and I'm so sorry." He tightened his grip on me, making it hard to breathe. I gave him a moment, until the discomfort became too much to bear, then gently pried him loose. He raised his face, cheeks wet, tears made orange by the lamplight, and looked at me with imploring eyes. "Can you forgive me?"

I stared down at him, the taste of his cock still on my tongue, and I wanted to vomit. I wanted to hurt him, to make those orange tears red. Instead, I said, "Yes. I can. If you can give me time."

He nodded, tried to smile. It looked pained. "Don't you want to know—?"

"No," I said sharply. "I don't want to know anything more than you've already told me. It's enough."

He leaned forward and put his face in his hands again. "You know I'd never hurt you on purpose. I love you, Gillian, and I promise you it'll never happen again."

I thought of us laughing earlier, of the warmth between us, and the feeling that everything was going to be all right, and then I imagined him fucking some stranger, and I felt cold spread through me. "I'm going downstairs," I said, and scoured the floor in the gloom for something to cover my nakedness.

"Do you want me to come with you?"

"No. You get some sleep. If you're still planning on going to work in the morning, you'll need it."

"I could stay home," he said, in his words the desperate need to know we were okay. But that was the last thing I wanted.

"No. Go. I need the time to myself."

"Gillian, you have to believe I'm sorry."

"Get some sleep, Chris. We can talk tomorrow."

"I'd rather talk about it now."

"No," I said, unable to keep the iciness from my tone. "You wouldn't."

There was nothing he could say to that, so that's what he said.

I located one of his dirty T-shirts and considered putting it on until it occurred to me that this, or any of the other clothes scattered around the floor might be what he had worn the night he had cheated on me. It might smell like the other woman, might have one of her hairs clinging to it. I flung the shirt aside and went into the bathroom and retrieved my robe from the hook on the bathroom door instead, then headed downstairs, leaving Chris alone with his guilt.

* * *

It was almost five in the morning. I was so tired the room around me jolted rather than moved when I turned my head, but I knew that sleep was unlikely to come. So, I sat up, tried to read a Tom Clancy novel Chris had started and given up on, but it wasn't long before I did the same. The words looked smudged, and only aggravated my headache. Next, I tried to eat, but managed only to lay some cold cuts on a plate before they began to look exactly like what they were: circular pieces of cold flesh. I stuck the laden plate back into the fridge and thought about drinking. Chris had left plenty of beer in the fridge, and though it was inadvisable for so many reasons, the idea appealed, as did the thought of a cigarette to accompany it. So, I fetched a beer, opened it, grabbed a cigarette from the pack Chris had left on the table, and settled down at the counter.

Sat. Put the cigarette in my mouth. Fingered the lighter, all to the faint sound of the beer's carbonated fizzing. Hesitated. I deserved the cigarette, didn't I, despite no real urge to have one? And the beer? Why not slam a few? After all, if I couldn't understand or empathize with Chris's motives for doing what he'd done, maybe I could at least get hammered enough to meet him at his level. And hey, maybe it would be enough to knock me into a dreamless sleep after I got done telling my husband what a backstabbing shit-for-brains he was.

I flicked the Bic, watched the sparks, ignited the flame, and quickly put it down when it occurred to me that I'd have gotten more satisfaction from burning the skin on my own fingers than the cigarette. I did, however, take a sip of the beer, and immediately grimaced. It tasted like the inside of an old shoe. I ran to the sink, spat out the rank liquid, rinsed out my mouth, gargled and then spat again. As I did so, a pulsing red light in the window above the sink caught my attention. At first my tired eyes mistook it for a light outside, perhaps the glowing cherry of a watcher's cigarette, but then I realized it was only the phone in the room behind me reflected in the glass, reminding me of the message.

I straightened, filled myself a glass of water, and went to the machine.

Thumbed the PLAY button.

After the phone's customary preamble telling me when the message had been recorded, an unfamiliar voice began to speak.

It was the police, and they'd called from my father's house after finding my number on his chair.

SIXTEEN

I DREAM.
I am in my father's house. The carpet is gone, replaced by long thick grass that dances in the breeze blowing through ragged, gaping holes in the walls. Outside, there is no neighborhood, only deep, impenetrable dark, though here, the ivy-covered walls glow with an ethereal viridescent light. The earth beneath the grass is loamy and wet; it squelches as I trod with bare, dirty feet through the rooms.

Rain taps with insistent fingers against the roof.

My father is not out there in the darkness, hooked hands ready to enter me and leave their filth inside. Even in sleep I know the days of hating and fearing him are over and that this will be the last dream of its kind. I am here to do what I refused to do in the waking world. I am here to see the body. This is the end of a long cruel journey, and I feel no apprehension now. I feel nothing. I am simply here.

As I navigate the hallway, from which long wet strips of wallpaper uncurl and slip to the floor and plaster rains in dust from the ceiling, the grass disappears, and I find myself ankle-deep in brackish water. My breath plumes in the air before my face as I reach the stairs and, without hesitation, put my hand on a balustrade made from polished human bone. The steps themselves are made of cold, damp earth that chill my feet and numb my toes as I ascend.

Portraits hang askew on the wall, having been clumsily nailed to it through both glass and frame. Each one shows a picture of my children at different ages, all in anachronistic black and white. Sam the newborn, screaming in panic after being tugged into this alien world like a fish on a hook. Jenny playing volleyball the first day of middle school, her face set with the same grim defiance she would master in later years. Sam on the front porch in an Ohio State University football shirt two sizes too big, arms akimbo, face-painted red and white, grinning at the novelty of it all. Jenny, sitting at the piano in music class, hands poised over the keys, the determination evident in her posture. She would quit trying to learn the instrument six months later, but no one would soon forget the tantrums that resulted during her attempts to prove she was smart enough to get it.

At the top of the stairs is a picture of Chris. We're at Niagara Falls, where we spent our honeymoon. He is wearing a blue shirt and khaki pants. I am wearing a white low-cut top and jeans, and smiling. Whether or not Chris is smiling is unknown because the rusty nail used to affix the picture to the wall has been driven through his face.

I round the corner. Before me is my room. The door is open and there is a little girl sitting on the bed, backlit by lurid-red neon light from a sign that hangs outside her window. She is dressed in her Sunday best, and twin trails of darkness run from her nose. Her head is bowed.

"Hello," I say, standing just short of the threshold to her room. I don't wish to disturb her, for the girl is disturbed enough, and I know she considers adults creatures not to be trusted, even if this one is her future self.

She doesn't respond, but her right foot jumps, as if kicking at something unseen, then is still again.

"I'm sorry," I whisper, "that I didn't know how to save us."

With no response forthcoming from the girl, from me, I move on.

Rainwater patters to the floor from cracks in the ceiling. It puddles here and there.

My brother's door is open too, and he is here also, sitting on the floor surrounded by toys. As I step inside, he looks up. There are dark circles beneath his eyes, and the side of his head is swollen, which pulls the flesh on his face taut, making it look like pictures I have seen of botched plastic surgeries.

He smiles crookedly at me. He is missing most of his teeth, and those that remain are stained with old blood. "Did you come to play?" *he asks.*

I shake my head and feel sorrow swell in my chest. God, I miss him.

"They turned the rocks a few days before," *John tells me. It is a line that I've heard before, not from him, but from our mother in the days after his death.*

They turned the rocks a few days before. They must have. Something they probably do before school starts. You children rolled down that hill hundreds of times and never got hurt. Someone must have done something.

"No," *I tell John.* "You know they didn't."

He looks at me, then away. "You know that now? The truth? I thought you quit listening."

"I'm learning how all over again."

"Good. And what does it tell you?" *He places his hand on a toy dump truck and rolls it across the floor. There are little men with no faces inside the cab, moving.*

"It tells me I did the right thing. The only thing I could do to help you."

"You hurt me. Even after you promised you wouldn't."

"I saved you, Jack."

He gives the truck a hard shove which sends it careening into the wall. "And what about what you're going to do? Who is that supposed to save? You? Or them?"

"I don't know what I'm going to do yet."

He gives me a cold grin. "Then you aren't really listening."

As he reaches for an old toy fire engine covered in what appear to be thick wriggling black worms, I leave him there and go to find my father.

The old man is in his room, though much like the rest of the house, it looks nothing like it did when I visited it in the real world. Instead, it has been decorated to resemble a parlor in a funeral home. All white-marble columns and mortuary light. At the far end of the room sits a slab draped in red velvet, and atop that slab is an oak coffin, the lid open wide to reveal the body resting within.

Despite the certainty that there is nothing to fear anymore, I nevertheless feel a twinge of discomfort and an unexpected pang of loss when I enter the room.

My father is dressed in a black suit. A handkerchief the color of fresh blood pokes like a tongue from the breast pocket. In a curious reversal, death has made him appear younger, though I suspect this might be attributable to the mortician's cosmetology skills, or perhaps the natural effect of being freed from the burden of life and, perhaps, the guilt. His hair has been neatly slicked back, his bushy eyebrows plucked and smoothened, and the red veins across his nose are gone.

As I place my hands on the edge of the coffin, I find myself wishing, even in this subconscious construct, that things had been different, that he had been my father in more than just title. Mostly, I wish he'd loved me and John like all good fathers love their children.

"I tried," he says then, and opens his eyes. "Every day I tried."

Slowly, his gaze moves to where I stand looking down upon him.

"Every day I promised myself I would stop. Sometimes, when I was sure your mother was asleep, I would confess to her, and beg for her forgiveness because I didn't have the guts to beg my children, or to seek help. But I tried."

"So, you knew?" I asked him. "You knew something was wrong with you?"

"Of course. I even confessed everything to Father Garrety, and you know what he said? He said, 'Seek counsel with Our Lord and Savior. He's the only one who can help you now.' How I wish it had been that simple."

"You could have gone for help."

"And risk having the whole town know?"

"They ended up knowing anyway, and might at least have given you some credit for trying to set right what was wrong with you. Some things are a little more important than pride. Your children, for one."

"I know, but I was weak." He closes his eyes. "In so many ways. And I'm sorry."

When he says nothing for a long time, I reach out and place my hand on his. His skin is cold.

"That's all I ever wanted to hear you say. Just to have you say it and know you meant it. It would have changed so many things between us. Not everything, not enough, but it would have made a difference."

When he speaks again, it is without opening his eyes. "But will you believe it? When you wake and have to accept that it's your words that are coming from my mouth, will it be enough?"

"I don't know."

He is silent then, just a dead body in a box, and all of it a dream.

As I head downstairs, I glance into the children's rooms. My younger self is sitting at a desk with her back to me, unmoving. John is playing with his G.I. Joe. The soldier is doing a victory dance over the corpse of a Barbie doll. I am struck with the unreasonable urge to bid them goodbye, for I know I will never see them again, not like this at least, but I don't. This is nothing more than a dream, a fabrication, a mental assemblage of sequences designed to reconcile fractured pieces of my history so that I can have a future.

No more words are needed.

I start down the stairs.

And stop.

My feet begin to sink into the mud.

A figure wades slowly through the water in the hall, stopping when he reaches the foot of the stairs. He is quivering, perhaps from the cold, more likely from excitement, the thrill of having trapped his quarry, and he raises his head to look at me as I stand frozen, spotlighted by the naked bulb above my head. He raises his arm, extending the rusted clothes hanger hook he has for a hand. A raindrop hits it, explodes and spatters the bag he wears over his head.

"I've done something I'm not proud of, honey," my husband says, as his grin crinkles the plastic.

SEVENTEEN

THE HEADACHE WAS THERE TO GREET ME in the morning, as were Chris and the kids. Chris made breakfast for me in what I took as a pathetic attempt to start making amends for his treachery. He needn't have bothered; my appetite was gone. I did, however, accept the coffee he placed before me.

"You get any sleep?" he asked.

I answered him with a look.

"You should take a nap later."

I noted then that he was dressed in a sweater and jeans. Also, he hadn't shaved. His jaw was shadowed with stubble, which only accentuated the hungover look.

"Thought you were going to work today?" I asked, my voice raspy and raw.

He looked at the kids, as if to gauge how much attention they were paying us before he answered. Jenny was intent on an issue of *Entertainment Weekly* and, naturally, listening to her iPod; Sam was studying whatever was written on the back of the Rice Krispies box as he slurped cereal from his spoon.

"I thought it would be better if I stayed at home," Chris said. "Give us a chance to talk."

"I don't much feel like talking," I told him, "which shouldn't come as a surprise."

He nodded his understanding. "Baby steps, then."

The rumble of an old engine followed by a loud pneumatic hiss from outside signified the arrival of the school bus. Chris seemed glad of the distraction, however brief it proved to be, and set about corralling the kids, unplugging one of Jenny's earbuds—much to her annoyance—to let her know it was time to leave. Sam was already off his chair and slinging on his book bag.

"C'mon, hurry," Chris said. "Before Mr. Jessop takes off." For some inexplicable reason, our district's bus driver gave the children a grace period of thirty seconds to appear on the porch or he'd leave without them. It was a process that had necessitated our driving the kids to school on many occasions, and the registering of more than one complaint from inconvenienced parents. I'd even spoken to Jessop—who was not nearly as cantankerous as his behavior and the testimony of the children suggested—and his defense was that to wait any longer meant that all the children would be late and therefore marked as tardy by their teachers, and he'd rather not have such a thing on his conscience.

"Wait," I said, and only Jenny was slow in giving me her attention.

"They're going to miss—" Chris started to say, and I waved away his words.

"I'll drive them."

The kids looked at each other, surprised.

"You sure?" Chris asked.

"Yes. I want to." I gave the kids as warm a smile as I could muster. "It's been a while since Mommy drove you guys, right?"

Sam nodded. Jenny shrugged.

The benefit for the kids of being driven to school was an extra forty minutes before they had to leave. For Sam, this meant a quick fix of cartoons; for Jenny, extra talk-time on her cell with her best friend Sarah.

Chris looked as if he wasn't quite sure what to do with himself now that the impetus of the morning had been stalled so unexpectedly. Hands on hips, he looked around the kitchen. I watched him for a moment, carefully, then pushed back my chair and rose. That caught his attention and he offered me a slight smile lit more by hope than affection.

"I'm going to take a shower," I said.

* * *

There was more than one ulterior motive behind my offer to drive the kids to school.

First, I wanted to get out of the house and away from Chris now that he had made the inconvenient decision to take the day off. I anticipated endless hours of him hovering around me, waiting for some small sign that I was willing to let him in, if only so he could plead his case sober after making the drunken mistake of confessing in the first place.

Secondly, I needed to talk to the children without their father present. And as I turned the truck out of our driveway, I looked at them both in the mirror.

"Sam, tell your sister to turn the music off. I need to talk to her."

I watched as he tugged on her sleeve. She jerked away from him. He poked her with a finger and she glared, bunched her fist to threaten him with a punch, until she saw my eyes in the mirror. She sighed, did not remove the ear buds, but turned the iPod off.

"What?" she said.

"I want to ask you a question."

"Okay, so ask."

"You too, Sam."

He said nothing, just looked at his sister, then back to the mirror.

I waited until the house was out of view, then slowed and angled the car into the long winding driveway of the Crescent View Horse Ranch. In the distance, backlit by the sun, the half-dozen or so horses out in the fields looked majestic. I sighed, killed the engine and turned around in my seat so I was facing the children.

"This isn't an easy question to ask, and it's not going to be an easy one for either of you to answer. But I want you both to know that even though I haven't been there for you much over the past few months, I'm here for you now, and you can tell me anything, no matter how bad. Ok?"

Sam nodded eagerly, excited by the mystery. Jenny frowned. "What's this about?"

The words crowded my head, alternate means of conveying such a terrible question suggesting themselves in a maddening rush until my headache began again. I massaged my temple with a trembling hand and closed my eyes for a moment, willing it to leave me be, if only for a little while.

"Mommy?" That was Sam's voice, filled with concern.

"I'm okay," I said. "Just a migraine."

"You should go to the doctor," Sam suggested. "He'll fix it."

I smiled, opened my eyes. "You're right, and I will."

That, I couldn't tell them, was a part of my promise to Chris I had decided to break. No doctors and no shrinks. I hadn't trusted them as a child, and I trusted them even less now. No adults could be trusted, period.

"Jenny..."

"What?"

I waited a beat as a car raced by, the wake of its passage enough to rock the truck.

"Wow, that was fast!" Sam said, turning around in his seat to see if the racer was still in sight. "Bet it was a Ferrari!"

"Jenny, does your father ever touch you?"

Puberty had made a cheerless, morose creature of Jenny. Regardless of whether she was happy or not, she looked solemn. That forced solemnity dropped now, replaced by genuine look of horror and embarrassment. "Why would you *ask* me that?"

Sam turned back to face us, alerted by the tone in his sister's voice.

"He may have told you it was okay for him to do certain things, but..."

Her face turned beet red. "Mom, stop."

"It's all right, honey. You can be honest with me. Has he ever touched you in a way that made you feel uncomfortable, or scared?"

Sam frowned. "What does that mean?"

I turned my attention on him. "It means being touched where you don't want to be. Like in your...your private area."

Sam giggled. "Gross!" The reaction seemed a little too genuine, too *him* to be forced, and that came as a relief. From Jenny, however, I got no such reassurance. She stared down at her hands, her face still flushed.

"Jenny, honey, tell me."

"Tell you what?"

"Does your father ever—"

"No!" she cried, slamming her palms on her knees. "No, and you shouldn't be asking sick questions like that. What's *wrong* with you?"

I gave her my best maternal smile. "It's natural to be angry, baby."

"I'm angry at *you!*" she screamed, hot tears spilling down her cheeks. "You've been acting crazy and you're scaring me and Sam."

I looked at Sam, and saw that she was right. He did look scared now, but no more than he always did when Jenny threw a fit. It was *she* who was angry, and, misdirected as it was, I fully understood that reaction. Hadn't I had nurtured the same flame inside myself my whole life? Who better then to recognize its nature and probable cause?

"I'm sorry," I said. "You're right. I just worry." The words were meant to pacify not persuade. I was beyond such deception now. Clearly, I would need to get Jenny alone before she would feel secure talking to me. Sam's presence only embarrassed her, and I realized I should have known that. She was a grown-up now, or so she liked to think. As such, it would be beneath her to admit anything in front of her younger sibling that might make her appear weak in his eyes.

I turned back in my seat and started the engine.

"Jesus," Jenny muttered, and I should have chastised her for that, but knew if I wished to gain her trust, it was better not to. Maybe as a footnote to a future conversation, but not here, and not now.

Sam gasped. "I'm telling!"

"She heard me, dummy." Jenny sneered.

I reversed the car onto the road.

It didn't matter whether Jenny ever admitted to what Chris was doing to her. I knew. *A woman knows*, I'd thought while watching Chris preparing his confession of adultery. I amended that now, because yes, a woman knows, but not nearly as much as a *mother* does. And if there were any gaps in my logic, they were filled with the evidence at my disposal.

Chris's words, repeated in the dream because I'd missed the implication when he'd said them the first time: "I've done something I'm not proud of, honey." Not, "I had an affair" or "I slept with another woman" or any of the myriad variations of the theme. The woman was never specifically mentioned at all. No names, no explanations of how the treachery had come to pass. No details. Because no details were necessary. What he had done, he'd done to *our* daughter, in *our* house, and he was not confessing to an affair, but a weakness, a lapse in restraining the very same disease that had inhabited my father.

In the dream, my brother had told me many things I had taken at face value rather than reading deeper into them. He was trying to tell me what was happening, what was coming. Or rather, some part of *me* was trying to warn me, using the image of my brother to convey the message for fear I wouldn't heed it if it occurred to me in the light of day.

Don't be a fucking idiot, sis. You know what he did, what he's doing still.

I had assumed he was talking about our father.

Then you aren't really listening.

And yes, perhaps I had only imagined Jenny sitting in her room when I'd gone to tuck her in that night, but now I knew the words she'd said had been real and not misheard. They had come from her dreams, where the truth can hold court with no lips to block it.

He touches me, Mommy.

The headaches, the nightmares, every awful thing I had seen or thought I'd seen...it could all be traced back to the moment Jenny began to blossom from a child into a young girl. She was now the age I'd been when hell had found me. The only difference was that I hadn't had anyone to protect me. And rather than face the reality of what was happening, I had obsessed over my pathetic father and his sins, even as my subconscious tried to show me the light.

"Mom, you went the wrong way," Sam piped up from the back seat.

He was right. Distracted by my thoughts, I had missed the turn.

I slowed the car, checked the rearview for traffic and caught sight of Jenny's eyes. They were moist, but she was no longer crying, and in them I saw a flicker of anger.

The flame.

I smiled.

That's my girl.

EIGHTEEN

I returned home after dropping off the kids to find the house quiet and Chris dozing on the couch. He had his face turned away, mouth open and snoring, arms crossed as if his falling asleep had been an act of petulance. He hadn't changed his clothes, which meant he hadn't showered, and as I knelt on the floor beside him, I detected the noxious smell of alcohol still seeping from his pores.

"You never knew so many things," I whispered, knowing he wouldn't wake. "Some, because of your ignorance and stupidity. Others, because I chose not to tell you. And I chose not to tell you because a part of me always suspected you had the darkness inside you, that I couldn't trust you no more than I could trust any grown-up." This, I realized, was why I hadn't told him about my visit to my father, or that the old man had died. Knowing that the object of my focus was gone, leaving him vulnerable to scrutiny, might have made Chris more careful, more cunning, and then I'd never have exposed him for what he was.

But a mother always knows.

I brought my hand close to his face, but did not touch it. I could feel the heat rising from his skin and wondered what feverish, perverse dreams were running through his head. What was he doing to Jenny in that dark theater behind his eyes? I withdrew my hand as if afraid the poison that coursed through his veins might leap out and infect me, and let my gaze wander down over his body from the cleft of his unshaven chin down over his throat, to the hairs curling out over the neck of his sweater, to his chest as it slowly rose and fell. Here I placed my hand, so that I could feel his heartbeat, and there it was, racing with excitement. At once, depraved images of my husband and my little girl tried to implant themselves in my head, pulsing into my brain in time with his heartbeat, and I quickly stood, my body quivering with repulsion. The flashes had been brief, but enough. His tanned, muscular body crushing her pale skin while she screamed against the hand he had clamped over her mouth. Her eyes wide with fear, glassy with disgust, self-loathing, and horror. And in her mind, the desperate hope that it would be over soon, that I would discover them and make it all better.

For only the briefest of moments I watched him, sleeping like a baby, like an innocent, before I hurried into the kitchen, fetched what I needed, and returned, tears streaming down my face. My skull became a cave roaring with the echoes of a thousand voices, all of them united in a singular chorus to drown out the only one not in tune. The one that screamed: *What if you're wrong?*

I told myself it was possible.

But then, anything was possible.

Thunder grumbled somewhere in the distance.

Sudden rain hit the window in a scattershot spray.

Chris twitched, moaned in his sleep.

And woke.

Jesus Christ, Gillian, stop. What if you're wrong? the lone voice whispered. It was not loud enough, not persuasive enough to make a difference, or to be heard above the ululating crowd, who now filled my head with their bloodlust song.

I could be wrong, I thought.

Chris opened his eyes, blinked and looked blearily up at me.

But I'm not.

"Honey?" he asked, a quaver in his voice as his confused gaze dropped to the knife I held tightly in one trembling hand. "What...what are you doing?"

Instantly, the voices fell quiet.

"What I should have done a long time ago," I told him, and plunged the knife into his stomach. Or rather, tried to. I had underestimated the amount of force necessary to drive the blade into him and managed only to penetrate a half inch or so of his flesh before he screamed and rolled off the couch, hit the floor, then quickly scrabbled to his feet. His eyes were glassy with terror.

"Gillian!" he cried, wincing and doubled over slightly in pain. "What the fuck are you *doing?*" Hands covering the small hole I'd made in him, he backed away from me. "What's the *matter* with you?"

Confused and shocked, he did not move fast enough as I quickly stepped close and slashed the knife across his face, narrowly missing his eyes. He cried out again, a deep vertical red line opening just beneath his eyelids and across the bridge of his nose. Stunned, he staggered backward, one hand now raised to probe the extent of the damage to his face. Blood ran freely down his cheeks, welled on the tip of his nose.

"You won't touch her ever again," I told him, and my voice sounded alien to my ears. Younger, perhaps, and angrier. The old me, the wounded me. The victim.

He raised his hands in surrender. "Gillian, honey...let me call someone. Let me get you some help. You're sick, but we can fix it."

I lunged forward, dodging his attempt to block me with a skill and agility of which I had not known myself capable, and thrust the knife into the meat of his right thigh with such force that the blade bent a little. Chris howled in agony, stumbled, and fell gracelessly to the floor.

"Gillian, my God, look at what you're *doing! Please*, baby..."

The hardwood was spattered with his blood. The right leg of his jeans had turned dark. The last wound had been a deep one, and with time, he might have bled out. But I was not willing to wait. Here before me, looking pathetic, afraid, and helpless, was a monster, crippled by defeat and the vengeance of an innocent. Felled by his own prey. No, I would not wait for him to die slowly, no matter how satisfying the thought.

"*Gillian...*" His face had become a monochrome portrait of horror and disbelief. I recognized that look. Had seen it in the mirror for most of my childhood. "Baby, *listen* to me...you have to stop. You don't know what you're doing."

"I know exactly what I'm doing."

He dragged himself backward with his hands. Patiently, ever-so-slowly, I followed, here and there answering his pleas for mercy, for clarity, with the blade, and by the time I was done, he had made it into the kitchen before the strength to go any further abandoned him.

"Why...?" he managed to ask. Blood continued to spread around him in an ever-widening pool from the dozen or so puncture wounds on his chest, face, arms and legs. With his resistance minimized, I'd managed—admittedly with great difficulty—to sever the tendon on the back of each foot, disabling him just in case the other wounds didn't. "Why did you do this to me? It was a mistake, that's all...that's *all* it was. A stupid mistake. Please, Gillian, *please* get help. I'm going to die." He began to sob.

"Yes, you are," I told him, and knelt between his legs, felt his blood soak through my jeans. It was warm and unpleasant, but I did not intend to have to endure it long. My hands were shaking violently, my head raging with myriad voices, as I undid the button on his jeans and unzipped him.

"Honey...no...Jesus..." he whined, every word punctuated by a sob. Feebly he tried to resist me, but he was in too much pain, had lost too much blood. He looked like the ghost I intended to make of him.

"Hush now," I whispered. "Someone will hear."

He tried to pull away from me as I grabbed his cock and put the edge of the blade beneath his testicles.

I imagined it impossible that no one heard the resulting scream. But such things were beyond my concern. Only the presence of my children at the door would have prevented me from finishing. At such a young age, they, or Sam at least, should be spared seeing such brutality, no matter how justified and necessary. It might warp them.

When it was done, I left Chris unconscious, fetched some string from the utility drawer and one of the deluxe freezer bags I kept for storing meat from the cabinet over the refrigerator.

It's over now, I thought, with something akin to relief and excitement, as I went to the monster's stricken body, got to my knees, and raised his head just enough to slip the freezer bag over it. Then I looped the string around his neck, cinching tight the edges of the plastic.

Then I stood and studied him.

His breath, slow and uneven, clouded the interior of the bag.

But only for a little while.

NINETEEN

I dream, but I am not asleep.
Instead, life has become the dream.
I am there again, on the hill overlooking Mayberry. At my back are the crosses, driven like stakes through mounds of earth, three of which cover people I have known and lost. Perhaps Chris should be here, but he is in his own place, feeding the walnut tree at the end of our yard from which Sam's tire swing hangs forgotten. Sooner or later I suspect his absence will be noted—already some woman named Clare from the bank has been calling the house—but for now at least, we are safe.

The children do not yet know Chris is gone, only that he is away. In time, it won't matter. They will deal with it with the same resiliency all children employ when they are forced to accept an unkind reality.

I have not yet seen the expected relief on Jenny's face, and to date (four days since I killed her tormentor), she insists that there was never anything awry in the relationship between her and her father. But this, I suspect, is the natural fear of reprisal should he ever return and discover that she has shared their dark secret. Eventually, she will confess, and I will be there to listen.

After I told Sam what my little brother and I used to do here, he immediately wanted to try the game for himself, and so I watch as he tumbles down the hill on a wave of laughter. It warms my heart to see it. My little Jack.

Jenny, of course, considers herself too mature for such things. She stands up there at the top of the hill watching Sam, just as on that last day, I watched John, my thoughts occupied with ways to help him escape the nightmare. I wonder what it is my daughter's thinking now. Is she pondering the benefits of her father's absence, or replaying the horrors he forced her to endure? The sun is sinking in the sky behind her, throwing the shadow of a lopsided cross down the hill toward where Sam is only now coming to rest, spread-eagled on the grass.

"That was awesome!" he cries.

I wish only the best for him, a good life free of the kind of terrors that infected Jenny's, and mine. And nightly I pray that he will never become the monster, for the corrupt elements are extant in all young men. I'll watch, and I will guide him, and I will protect them both. And should the day ever come in which it becomes necessary to save them, then I will do that too.

It is my duty as a mother.

As for me, I sit at the foot of the hill on the low wall across from the school with its dark windows, reading the *Mayberry Times* newspaper. It is filled with accounts of the mundane: break-ins, altercations, traffic violations, political treachery, but nothing that bears further study. And this is good. Because I know, as every mother should, that there are still monsters here, as there are everywhere, but for now at least, they are quiet.

ABOUT THE AUTHOR

Born and raised in a small harbor town in the south of Ireland, Kealan Patrick Burke knew from a very early age that he was going to be a horror writer. The combination of an ancient locale, a horror-loving mother, and a family full of storytellers, made it inevitable that he would end up telling stories for a living. Since those formative years, he has written five novels, over a hundred short stories, six collections, and edited four acclaimed anthologies. In 2004, he was honored with the Bram Stoker Award for his novella *The Turtle Boy*.

Kealan has worked as a waiter, a drama teacher, a mapmaker, a security guard, an assembly-line worker at Apple Computers, a salesman (for a day), a bartender, landscape gardener, vocalist in a grunge band, curriculum content editor, fiction editor at *Gothic.net*, associate editor at *Subterranean* magazine, and, most recently, a fraud investigator.

When not writing, Kealan designs book covers through his company Elderlemon Design.

A number of his books have been optioned for film.

Visit him on the web at www.kealanpatrickburke.com

KEALAN PATRICK BURKE

NOW AVAILABLE in DIGITAL and PAPERBACK

BLANKY

In the wake of his infant daughter's tragic death, Steve Brannigan is struggling to keep himself together. Estranged from his wife, who refuses to be inside the house where the unthinkable happened, and unable to work, he seeks solace in an endless parade of old sitcoms and a bottle of bourbon.

Until one night he hears a sound from his daughter's old room, a room now stripped bare of anything that identified it as hers...except for her security blanket, affectionately known as Blanky.

Blanky, old and frayed, with its antiquated patchwork of badly sewn rabbits with black button eyes, who appear to be staring at the viewer...

Blanky, purchased from a strange old man at an antique stall selling "BABY CLOSE" at a discount.

The presence of Blanky in his dead daughter's room heralds nothing short of an unspeakable nightmare that threatens to take away what little light remains in Steve's shattered world

Because his daughter loved Blanky so much, he buried her with it.

A new novella from the Bram Stoker Award-Winning author of SOUR CANDY and KIN.

Printed in Great Britain
by Amazon